CHAOS
& the Geek

ALSO BY ELIZABETH STEVENS
NEW ADULT/ADULT BOOKS
Heaven & Hell Chronicles
Damned if I do
Damned if I don't
Damned if I know
All Devilbums Go To Heaven

Grace Grayson Security
Chaos & the Geek
Hawk & the Lady
O Lord & the Queen
Rollie & the Rocker
Tank & the Rebel

Loving the Sykes
Caden
Carter
Luther
Oscar
Ashton

MATURE YA/NEW ADULT BOOKS
the Trouble with Hate is…
Accidentally Perfect
Gray's Blade
Being Not Good
Popped

a **GRACE GRAYSON** novel

CHAOS

& the Geek

ELIZABETH STEVENS WRITING AS

PIPPA LANGHORN

KINKY
SIREN

Kinky Siren
An imprint of Sleeping Dragon Books

Chaos & the Geek
by Pippa Langhorn

Print ISBN: 978-1925928174
Digital ISBN: 978-1925928167

Cover art by: Izzie Duffield

Worldwide Electronic & Digital Rights
Worldwide English Language Print Rights

To the Duffields,
with love from Glitorus Clittertits.

♥

Contents

Amber 1
Kit 23
Amber 39
Kit 52
Amber 62
Kit 77
Amber 90
Kit 103
Amber 120
Kit 131
Amber 148
Kit 166
Amber 178
Kit 188
Amber 202
Kit 215
Amber 230
Kit 244
Chaos & the Geek 258
Thanks 259
My Books 260
About the Author 261

Author's Note

This book is written using Australian English. This will affect the spelling, grammar and syntax you may be used to. It might come across as typos, awkward sentences, poor grammar, or missed/wrong words. In the majority of cases (I won't claim it's infallible, despite all best efforts), this is intentional and just an Aussie way of speaking (it took my US beta readers a bit to get used to). I can't say 'the' Aussie way, since we seem to differ even within the same state. Just think of us as a weird mix of British and US vernacular and colloquialisms, but with our own randomness thrown in. I still hope you enjoy it, though!

1
Amber

I struggled with the lock as I juggled the books in my arms.

"Celebrate good times!" I called as I finally got the damned thing open and realised there was music blaring from Dannie's bedroom.

I kicked the front door closed, dropped my stuff on the couch and grooved along to the music. I wasn't usually so animated, especially after pulling an all-nighter at the library. But as I'd said, that day was cause for celebration. Getting totally shit-faced and karaoke-level celebration.

I grabbed the handle of my best friend's bedroom door.

"Break out the champers, lovely. We have– Oh, my bad," I laughed as Dannie tumbled off the guy she was riding enthusiastically.

My laughter died as Brent sat up from under her in complete shock like he'd been the one who'd just walked into the room. Dannie twirled around, grabbing the sheets to her like I hadn't seen her naked a hundred times over the years. And the shock and horror I felt on my face was mirrored on hers.

It took my brain a moment to work that I was actually seeing this. It took me a moment to stop trying to convince myself that I was just overworked and hallucinating – it had been known to happen, just not quite to this extent.

"Babe. It's not what it looks like…" Brent started, reaching for me.

"Really?" I blinked. "That's all you've got for me?"

Because, yep. The girl I'd been best friends with for almost twenty years was just having sex with my boyfriend. Admittedly, Brent and I hadn't been dating long. I guess. Is five months a lot these days? And we hadn't gone all the way. Yet. But I was busy dammit. Busy and stressed and Brent had said he didn't mind.

"Amber…" Dannie started and I shook my head.

"No." I closed my eyes and took a breath, feeling oddly numb. "Just… Please tell me this is the first time."

There was silence and I opened my eyes slowly to look at them.

"Babe, sure. It's the only time." Brent nodded. He was totally stealing the Razzie off Sly Stone this year for that dismal performance.

But Dannie would never lie to my face and the look on hers now told me all I needed to know. Something was starting to push through the numbness. I just wasn't sure yet if it was pain, sadness, or anger.

"How long?" I whispered.

Dannie grimaced. "Too long."

"What else were we supposed to do while we were

waiting for you to get out of that fucking boring library?”
Brent asked, obviously on the defensive.

“Oh, I don’t know! Not fucking each other? Literally any
of humanity’s numerous and varied other past-times but
fucking each other!” I snapped and I watched Brent’s eyes
go wide. Yes, I’d never said that word before, let alone
twice. “Now it makes sense why you were happy to wait…”

I took a deep breath and exhaled. Honestly I didn’t want
to argue with them about who was to blame or whether it
was right or wrong. So I turned and headed for my room. I
heard them yelling at each other, but I tuned them out as I
found my suitcase and started shoving as much into it as I
could.

“Amber!” Dannie called and I just shook my head.
“Amber, listen to me. It was an accident–”

I shook my head. “No. An accident is running over the
neighbour’s cat, Dan. Not sleeping with your best friend’s
boyfriend. I know I’ve been pulling ridiculous hours. But
am I not worth some loyalty and honesty? Any?” I yelled as
I slammed my suitcase lid down. I let out a breath, still not
sure what I was feeling…if anything.

I was starting to think any emotion was going to be too
scary so I didn’t want to name any.

“Of course you are. And we should have…”

“What?” I scoffed as I wrestled with my zipper. “Told
me? Or just not done it in the first place? I know he wasn’t
perfect, Dan. I knew he wasn’t Prince Charming. But I
really liked him. Especially after…”

I couldn't say it, but she'd been there through all of it. She didn't need the reminder any more than I did.

"I know, babes. I'm sorry."

I could only shake my head as I pulled the handle on my suitcase and shoved past her. Brent's betrayal was a non-issue; I'd liked the guy but he was just a guy. Dannie on the other hand? It was nice to know that, after everything we'd been through together, twenty years of best-friendship meant less than some guy's dick.

"Babe!" Brent called as I walked past Dannie's room, but I kept going.

I grabbed up my satchel and my books from the couch and my keys.

"Where are you going to go?" Dannie asked.

I paused, my hand on the doorknob. "I don't know. Anywhere's better than here."

I stormed out and headed for the lift. The old, rickety lift I hated. But I was so not bouncing my suitcase down ten flights of stairs. I breathed out heavily as the door closed on me and wasn't sure if I was staving off tears or the desire to punch something.

I hadn't had this complete numbness for so long. But it was like my body recognised it all too well and welcomed it with open arms like a long-lost limb. I stumbled a little as I walked out of the lift and headed for the rarely used back door in case I was followed. I was so busy ignoring any and all feelings that I didn't notice that the heavens that had been threatening to open all week had done just that with gusto until water ran into my eye.

I blinked and just stood there for a moment, not sure if I was crying now or not.

I don't know how long I was standing there, but I slowly registered that there was someone yelling. I focussed my eyes and saw a vaguely familiar older guy hurrying over the road towards me, calling to me.

He stopped in front of me and I blinked heavily.

"Are you all right, miss?" he asked and I realised he was familiar because he was wearing the uniform for the swanky place across the road.

I'd walked past enough times in the three years I lived there that I was sure I'd seen him at the door more than once.

"Miss? Are you okay?"

I shook my head out of my arse. "Um… I'm…" I looked back up to where I knew our apartment was. "I will be. Thanks."

"Have you got anywhere to go, miss?" he asked sweetly.

I smiled at him softly and shook my head. "No. I need to get hold of my brother. But then I'll be fine." I didn't know why I felt like I was about to divulge my whole life story to this lovely older gentleman, but he just had that trusted grandfatherly quality to him.

He gave me a sympathetic smile. "Why don't you come on over into the dry, miss? We can get you a hot drink and get hold of your brother for you?"

My eyes slid to the ridiculously expensive building across the road. "Thanks. But I'd hate to put you out and I wouldn't really fit in." I flapped my soaking oversized woollen jumper as evidence.

He made a tutting noise and winked at me. "I won't tell if you won't."

I saw his name tag read Johnson.

The idea of somewhere dry to call my brother from sounded amazing. And just then, I was incapable of thinking of anywhere else. So I finally nodded, let him take my case, and let him lead the way back across the road.

"Thank you, Johnson."

"You're most welcome, miss. I hated to see such a sweet young lady looking so lost. What's your poison? Tea? Coffee? Chocolate?" he asked as we hurried under the giant awning and he carried my bag up the steps.

"God, a stiff coffee would do me wonders."

"I'll ask the boys to throw in a fortifying shot of Jamesons," he said with a wink and a tap to his nose.

"It's a bit early in the day isn't it?" I *had* been joking.

"I won't tell if you won't," he said again as he directed me to some seats in the foyer. "Now, give me two ticks to find you a couple of towels and get the boys on that coffee, and we'll get you settled."

I nodded, starting to feel too overwhelmed to do much more. I pulled my phone out of my wet jeans and looked for my brother's number. It rang out and I couldn't think of what to say to his answering service, so I hung up and waited for Johnson to come back.

Just as that overwhelmed sensation was turning into self-pity and sadness, I saw Johnson jogging back over with some towels and a comforting smile.

"Here you go, miss. Dry off as best you can. Coffee's on the way."

"Thank you."

I took the top towel hesitantly as Johnson put the rest of the pile down on a chair beside us. The Mayhew was some kind of apartment/hotel complex that would cost more per night than a month of my rent. The towels were embossed with The Mayhew's emblem and were so soft I could have just snuggled up to them and fallen asleep. I rubbed myself over vigorously, only just realising I was shivering from cold.

"Anything else I can do, miss?"

I shook my head. "No, thank you. You've already done more than enough."

"All right. I'd best hop on back to work, then. The boys will bring your coffee when it's done. On me." He gave me that friendly wink again.

"Thank you, Johnson."

He gave me a little salute and strode back to the front doors.

I grabbed one of the dry towels and put it on the great wingback chair before I sat down and tried my brother again. I knew that calling him was the best way to get hold of him. He was the sort of guy who didn't pay attention to his phone unless it was making incessant noise. His notification tone just wasn't long enough and he still had an unread voicemail I'd let him four years ago.

But still no answer. Knowing he was probably working, I resolved to just try again later.

A nice young guy brought my coffee over and asked if I needed anything else, to which I assured him I was fine. He didn't look completely pleased I was there, but I assumed that had more to do with the fact that he didn't want to cop any flack for dishevelled little me being there than he was feeling superior.

I sat in my own corner of the world, my hand wrapped around the warmth of the mug, the Jameson sending a pleasant burn through me, and trying to get hold of my brother. Finally, he picked up.

"Sorry, Bert. You've only got like two minutes. What's up?" Patrick answered.

That was my loving brother. Okay if I was completely honest, he was incredibly loving. He just worked a seriously hectic job and I was lucky to get any time to talk to him, let alone see him. But it was preferable to him jaunting around the world on top secret barely-not-suicide missions in the name of other people's safety.

"I need a ride when you've got time?" I hedged.

"Time?" he scoffed, but I knew he was berating himself, not me. "Where do you need a ride to?"

"Anywhere that isn't near Dannie or Brent."

"Why?" his voice was hard. "What happened?"

"Let's just say, Dannie sampled my boyfriend before I did," I replied wryly.

"I will rip that ungrateful fucker a new one!" he growled.

"All right. Settle down, tiger. Do you have time to get me or not?"

He grunted as he thought. "You don't want to call Farrah…?"

Damn him knowing me so well. "I just figure it'll be weird with Dannie involved. I just need some space."

"You sound like you're holding up remarkably well?"

"I'm ignoring it."

"Bert, you can't do that."

"I can while I'm sitting in the foyer of the swankiest place this side of town," I hissed.

"Fuck!" he snapped and I wondered what had happened. "Wait. You're at the Mayhew? Okay. I can grab you in about…an hour?"

"You sure?"

"Yeah. I'll get Rollie or Tank to cover for me. It'll be fine. It's nothing big anyway." I heard him pause, but my brain had shorted out and I didn't respond. "Amber?" he pressed.

"I… Uh… You know what…?" I mumbled. I wasn't going to be able to wait an hour.

"Shit. I gotta go. I'll see you in an hour. Love you!" he yelled and I was listening to dial-tone while the first feeling broke through my numb defence. And of everything that had happened that morning, the only thing I felt was panic.

I felt like the world had suddenly fallen into slow motion as a tall, lean man in a light grey suit, black shoes, white shirt and black tie jogged down the stairs at the other end of the foyer. He was a specimen of true beauty, his suit tailored to perfection as his eyes passed over the foyer like a king surveying his kingdom. He kicked his chin in greeting to the lady at the front desk as his feet lightly touched the floor. He ran his hand through almost-black hair, that had been shorter last time I'd seen him, as he strode purposefully across the foyer towards where the guy with the coffee had come from.

Nearly eight years and he still had that alpha-male look about him, that ridiculous confidence that made girls seven years younger than him drool all over him. And I was indeed speaking from experience. He'd always been hot, but the last eight years had been kinder to him than they had to me. I'd seen a few pictures from his and my brother's military days, but those combat outfits had nothing on a tailored suit.

As he disappeared into the other room, I finally managed to remember how to breathe and let myself think his name.

Christopher Grayson.

Kit to his friends and family.

The guy my brother had nicknamed Chaos in junior school because of all the shit he got up to and later for all the hearts he left behind. He and my brother had been joined at the hip since they met in Reception. Then his family had moved down the street to mine when the boys were about ten and life for my brother had never been the same. He and Kit had been inseparable through school, a couple of years of uni, enlisting in the Navy, training and then both being hand-picked for some special ops team those left at home were never to be told about.

I'd never been able to look at Kit unless he didn't know I was in the room. I'd never been able to talk to him. Even without the seven-year age gap, I'd been a total mess around him. He'd been the first guy I'd crushed on and – if we're being honest – the only guy who'd ever starred in my dirty fantasies…or any fantasies really. He dated the most beautiful girls and got up to all kinds of things I'd probably never know about.

Even if we were to take away the whole sopping oversized jumper, the glasses, the frizzy hair and the tear-stained face thing, Kit Grayson was so far out of my league I wouldn't even be given clearance to clean in his league. Not that it mattered, because Kit Grayson had never noticed me past the awkward, weirdo little sister of his best mate and I'd gone to pains to keep it that way.

Except now he was in the room across the foyer and I still had to wait for my brother.

I checked the time. I'd stopped talking to Patrick about ten minutes before, so only fifty minutes. If that was a bar or restaurant, the likelihood of Kit being any less than that was slim. If he was less, it would be significantly less surely, and he wouldn't recognise me. Mind you, even if he did, he wasn't going to acknowledge my presence. So I was fine.

I kept telling myself I was fine as I kept an eye on the time and watched the hour pass and still no sign of my brother. I was starting to pray to anyone that Kit stayed in that room as I threw panicked looks between the front door and the room Kit disappeared into.

Another half hour, and still nothing as I kept a worried eye on both doors.

Then, because the world loved to kick me when I was down, I just registered that my brother walked in the front door as my eyes slid to the other door and I saw Kit walk out of the room.

My heart stammered to a stop and I actually stood up like that was going to somehow stop the train wreck I could see forming in front of me.

I muttered to myself as my gaze flickered between both men. "No. Please, no. If you were going to grant me anything. Do not let Christopher Barrett Grayson see me like this. I know I will never have a chance in hell with him, but some dignity after everything would be swell..." I mumbled as I watched them both inconveniently turn to each other and a flash of recognition crossed Kit's face.

"Hawk?" Kit called and my brother raised a hand in greeting.

Oddly, Kit's expression then dropped into a frown as they strode towards each other. I couldn't see my brother's face as they met and got into what looked like a very serious discussion until my brother shook his head. For the first time in my entire life, I watched as Kit's face fell into surprised confusion, then his eyes started roaming. And I was still standing up like an idiot.

Kit's eyes finally fell on me and there was no avoiding

the train wreck now.

I watched Kit nod in my direction, and my brother turned. The unfamiliar stress on his face melted as he saw me. He hurried over, but I could barely keep my eyes off Kit no matter how much I tried to make them stay.

"Bert. You okay?" my brother asked as he wrapped me up in his arms.

"I… Can we not talk about it now, Pat?" I replied, my eyes finally sliding off Kit entirely in awkwardness.

Patrick pushed me to arm's length and looked at me. "Chaos won't let me out of the meeting this afternoon, but I can drop you? Or you can take the car?"

I blinked, hoping to everything that was holy that my cheeks weren't as red as they felt. Like a complete dweeb, I pushed my glasses up my nose. "Whatever's better. But I can't stay with you—"

"Stay?" Kit asked. "Why would she need to stay with you?"

His voice hadn't lost any of that deep, gravelly quality that slid over your skin like a forbidden caress. And forbidden is exactly what he would have been had I even registered on his radar, so I cleared my throat to answer. But Patrick got in ahead of me.

"She's moving out of her place."

"Right now?" Kit asked and I watched his eyes glance down at my suitcase.

I nodded and – *for the love of God, Amber!* – pushed my glasses up my nose again. "Yeah. Right now. Left lots of my stuff behind, right now."

"Too right, too. If I see that fucker, I'm going to drag him to the deepest, darkest fucking hole in the fucking world," Patrick growled. And I was pretty sure he'd had one of those when the boys were special ops.

"What happened?" Kit snapped with this weirdly business-like efficiency.

"Amber's just walked in on her roommate – you remember Dannie? – and boyfriend fucking."

I grimaced as I looked around. "Language, Pat," I whispered, avoiding the look Kit shot me.

Despite how angry my big brother was about my boyfriend and best friend sleeping with each other behind my back, he sniggered. "You priss."

I wrinkled my nose at him, as antagonistic as I ever got. "Just goes to show a nice suit does not a gentleman make."

Patrick smirked. "And good manners does not a lady make."

"Regardless, if you haven't got time to take me to Mum and Dad's–"

"Ah, not so much. You can hang at mine?"

I wrinkled my nose in disgust. "Um. I've just pulled an all-nighter–"

"I can tell," Patrick chuckled.

"You can shut up," I mumbled as I looked at Kit out of the corner of my eyes. "I just need a hot shower and a sleep. And I'm not sleeping in your bed, thank you."

I knew what he got up to in his bed and not even clean

sheets was going to make me go anywhere near it.

"I have a perfectly suitable couch," Patrick said, pretending to be affronted.

"Your couch is for show, Pat. I'm not sleeping on that again without…how much was it?"

"Half a case of beer," he sniggered.

I nodded, "Yeah, that," and snuck a look over to see Kit's eyebrow rise in surprise.

Patrick chuckled again. "Okay. Well, you'll have to take the car–"

"I am *not* driving that monster again! You remember how much paint you lost last time?" I said, panicking.

Patrick's grin was merciless. "Yes. I do. And Chaos will well remember the bill he had to pay for it."

Now, I know I flushed as my eyes slid over to Kit again.

"She can stay with me," was all he said and it took me a moment to realise what those words had actually been implying.

"What?" I asked as Patrick looked half-way between shocked and pleased, and said, "You sure?"

I was staring straight at Kit's face, in close proximity, in a way I had never done ever. God, his eyes were still that deep, rich brown.

Kit shrugged. "Why not? I've got plenty of space and I'm barely there." He looked to me and I could only hold his gaze for less than a millisecond. "You can get meals up or go to the restaurant whenever you like. It'll be like living alone most days."

Restaurant? Meals up? He didn't live at the Mayhew did he?

"Chaos, mate. You seriously sure?" Patrick asked in that way he had where I knew he was about to say yes for me like I was still thirteen and incapable of making my own choices.

I blinked but no words wanted to come out.

I could *not* live with Kit Grayson. It was bad enough waking up from a dirty dream where he'd had his hands all over me. I couldn't actually see him. In person. In his house.

"Sister of my brother," he said as though that explained everything. "Amber's free to stay as long as she wants."

"Done. Thanks, man," Patrick laughed and I opened my mouth completely pointlessly as they shook hands. "Now, I'll have more excuses to see you," he said happily as he looked at me.

Why was all I was doing nodding dumbly? I had so many questions. More objections. But nodding seemed all I was capable of.

"We can take her up now and then head off?" Kit asked, sounding like he couldn't really care less about me now Patrick's crisis was over.

I nodded. "Yeah. Sure."

"Sweet!" Patrick nodded.

He grabbed my suitcase as Kit strode powerfully over to the lady at the front desk.

It seemed like all those years had not dulled his effect on the female species.

She – her name tag read Sally – batted her eyes at him. "How can I help you Mr Grayson?" she cooed, her eyes taking in me and Patrick and the suitcase.

"I need another key to the lift for my friend," he said curtly, pointing at me.

Sally baulked and I was willing to bet in however many years Kit had lived here he had never asked for a second key. And if he had, it wouldn't have been for a woman. I'd bet everything I owned. And just at that moment, that wasn't very much.

But she was a professional and she did as he asked. She got a card out and did something with a machine before sliding it over to him with a coquettish smile. Kit only nodded perfunctorily to her and kicked his head for us to follow him.

For some reason, I looked behind me and saw Johnson at the door. He gave me an encouraging smile and a wave. Then, there was a refraction of light off the door beside him and he was gone by the time my eyes cleared.

I followed my brother and his best friend into the lift. There was a guy standing in there in the Mayhew's uniform who nodded to Kit, but otherwise ignored us. As the doors closed, Kit held the key up to me in two fingers and I took it, careful not to touch his skin with mine.

"Press the 'P', then swipe the card at that panel," he instructed in that curt tone that I guessed meant he was already regretting this.

I did as he said and the lift must have been moving

because the numbers started scrolling. It was nothing like the lift I'd lived with for three years, which rattled and clanged and jerked you around so much you got whiplash.

Patrick nudged me. "Fucking nice, having your own key," he muttered as though it was some great conspiracy. "Me and the boys need Donald here to let us up."

"Yeah, well. If she's living there she'll want more freedom to come and go than I'm willing to let you wankers have," Kit shot back at him.

Finally, the numbers stopped and the doors slid open.

"Have a nice day, Mr Grayson," Donald said.

Patrick started wheeling my suitcase out and Kit went to follow him, then stopped.

"Ah. Don, this is Amber Grace. She's going to be staying with me for the foreseeable future."

I know we both saw the surprise on Donald's face at the word 'foreseeable'. It made me feel something too, I just wasn't sure what.

"Don't worry, Donald!" Patrick called. "She's just my sister. Player's still gonna play!" I heard him chuckle to himself.

Donald got control over his facial expression and nodded to me. "Pleasure to meet you, Miss...?" As usual, someone was having trouble believing Grace could be a last name.

"Grace, yes," Kit said.

Donald nodded again. "Miss Grace."

"Likewise," I said, then followed Kit out of the lift.

"What room do you want her in?" Patrick yelled as I

looked around in shock.

"South," Kit replied, then they both wandered in different directions, leaving me gaping like a fish.

I'd expected to exit the lift in a hallway like was normal. And I suppose in a way this was a hallway. It just happened to be a private hallway like Mum and Dad's front hall and opened out into a huge open plan room that ended in what looked like floor-to-ceiling, wall-to-wall windows. I hesitantly walked forward as I took in everything.

The penthouse – because what else did 'P' stand for? – was painted in fresh white with grey accents in various shades, smattered with metallic shines of copper and dark iron here and there. It was minimal living at best.

Kit's couches looked even less comfortable than Patrick's and the huge fire under the even bigger TV suggested this room wasn't used so much as it was meant to be admired. I felt like I'd fallen into one of the most expensive lifestyle magazines on the planet.

A noise to my left made me look at a huge galley kitchen where Kit was standing at a coffee machine. The cupboards were white and the top was white-flecked black granite or marble or something. The dining table was huge as well – a great glass and metal construction with dark grey upholstered chairs to sit at least twelve.

But it was the view that got me. I found myself at the window and had to stop myself pressing my hands against the glass. The room faced the opposite side of the building than the road across which I'd lived until a few minutes ago.

And under us was serious beauty. It was still early enough that the sun was on its climb over the buildings and shining off the struts of the huge bridge across the river in the background. On either side of the river, grass and trees spread out and I could just make out people hurrying about their days.

"Carmel will clean whatever hand prints she finds," a smooth voice said to my left and I snuck a look up at Kit.

He was holding a mug out to me and I took it, not caring if it was to my taste or not.

"It's beautiful," I said softly.

He nodded, staring over all that beauty while I took a moment to stare unabashedly at his. "It is."

"And you thought my place was sweet, Bert," Patrick said and I turned to look at him with a small smile.

"It is something."

"Hey, where's *my* coffee?" my brother glared at his best mate.

"Kitchen," Kit replied then turned his attention back to me. "We're going to have to head out soon. I don't know when I'll be back. But make yourself at home–"

"Fuck knows someone should," Patrick laughed.

Kit turned his patented brooding glare on him. "Sure. Anyway, there's an en suite to your room. Carmel stocks all the bathrooms with basics in case the team stay over. Use whatever you want. If there's anything you can't find, my bedroom's through those doors. Bathroom's the door on the right. Help yourself." He looked down as he pulled his phone out of his pocket, which was vibrating. "Hawk, can you show her to her room?" He nodded to me then answered the phone, "Grayson," and walked away.

"Come on, then. He'll be antsy to get going when he's done."

Patrick led me to the opposite side of the penthouse than Kit's bedroom – probably for the best – and down a hallway.

"So there's a study of sorts down this way. I know you like using the kitchen table, but it's there if you want it."

"Shouldn't I ask Kit first?"

"Nah, it's a spare. His office is over the other side. Don't worry about anything, Chaos and I will take care of it, okay?"

I nodded absently as he waved his arm through a door and I peeked in. "And all this because it was Champers Day," I sighed as I took in the huge room that I was supposed to call mine.

"What do you mean? Champers Day?" Patrick asked, following me into the room.

There were a couple of doors along one wall, two bedsides and a giant bed covered in plush pillows and covers, a chest of drawers next to the door, and a huge window between me and a balcony. There was a TV above the chest of drawers. Otherwise, the room was basically empty.

"Bert?" Patrick pressed.

I blinked. "Oh, I got my first chapter finished. My supervisor loved it," I huffed. Like it mattered anymore. My world had imploded and my thesis just felt so unimportant right then.

"What?" Patrick asked and pulled me to face him. "That's amazing!"

I gave him a sorry excuse for a smile. "That's why I was working all night–"

"Bert, let's not pretend you don't do that far too often."

My smile grew. "Yeah, okay. But I wanted to get it finished before our meeting and she loved it. It's by no means perfect yet, but for a draft she loved it."

Patrick hugged me. "We'll do Champers Day…" I heard him frown.

"As soon as you're free," I finished for him.

"Yes. I'll ask the boss for some time off."

"Hawk!" the boss in question called from the other room.

"Right, duty calls. I'll call you later?"

I nodded. "I'll be fine."

He looked me over carefully, but obviously my mask was solid. "Sweet." He kissed my forehead. "See you later."

"Bye."

He hurried out and I looked around my new room with a sigh.

"I'll be fine," I told myself.

2
Kit

What the fuck had I done?

The favour for Hawk was nothing. I was more than happy to help my best mate's little sister out of a jam. But Amber hated me. As in capital 'H' hated. Always had and I'd never known why. I knew it didn't help that I never knew how to talk to her.

Girls I didn't have a problem with.

It was just one girl.

One super sweet, totally good, crazy serious, studious girl who'd had no time for Hawk and my shenanigans at any age. A girl who'd ignored me or frowned at me and had probably said fifty words directly to me her whole life. She'd been a major part of my life since she was born and I couldn't picture it without her existing, but we on no level got along. We did not get along to the extent that we hadn't seen each other in something like eight years despite the fact I worked with her brother and our parents saw each other at least weekly. My dorky little brother – who thought he was basically Chaos 2.0 – saw her more often than I did.

And eight years had done a lot for little Amber Grace. She'd been sixteen when I'd really seen her last, barely entering womanhood. But you could see, even then, that she was going to be a looker. Admittedly, soaking wet in an oversized jumper and her glasses fogging up, she was doing an excellent job of hiding it. But she still had something about her that didn't need an expensive dress, perfect makeup, or actual sleep to be beautiful. And she always had.

When she wasn't obviously disapproving of me and Hawk, she'd always managed to intimidate me with how smart and confident she was. But she was still my best mate's little sister. Offering up my place had been second-nature. I hadn't even thought about it. I definitely had the space – why had I bought a place with four bedrooms and two offices? Because I could.

It'd be fine. I was barely there, work saw to that. I basically only saw what I'd spent a huge chunk of money on the way to my bed and on the way out again. So Amber and I wouldn't have to see each other, but I'd know she was safe and comfortable. I could work with that. And I had nothing against her. I just didn't know what to do in the face of her blatant indifference.

Hawk whacked me and I blinked.

"Where the fuck are you today?" Tank asked with a chuckle.

"He's probably trying to work out if he left the handcuffs out after he told Bert to help herself to his bathroom," Hawk chuckled and I frowned at them all.

I hadn't left the handcuffs out. I never left the handcuffs out. I never left anything out. Years in the military had ensured that everything had its proper place and it was kept there.

Rollie leant forward, leaning on the table. "Why is Amber being told to help herself to Chaos' bathroom?" He cocked his head sideways in that unnerving bird-like manner he had.

None of the boys had met Amber, but Hawk talked about her all the time. She'd been the main thing to get him through every mission we'd gone on; he'd never been able to bear the idea of not going home to her. And that had kept my arse in gear because I also couldn't bear the idea of her losing him.

For a seven year age gap and seemingly nothing in common, they were crazy close. Hawk was constantly talking to her between jobs and from his office. You could always tell when he was on the phone to Amber and when he was talking to anyone else; when he laughed, you gave him as much time as you could.

"She's staying with me," I said, rearranging in my seat. "Now can we get back to the Fortescues?"

"No," Nico said simply from behind his computer.

"She came home to find Dannie fucking her boyfriend," Hawk explained and the other three gasped like we were fifteen year old girls gossiping crushes. "So she packed up a suitcase and left. We bumped into Chaos in the lobby and he very kindly offered up one of his many spare rooms."

"Wait. I thought you hated Amber?" Rollie asked, grinning around his pen.

I shook my head and rearranged again. "I never hated her. We just never–"

"Speak. Acknowledge each other. Get along," Hawk offered and I glared at him.

"The Fortescues?" I tried.

"No," Nico said again.

"She's staying with me as long as she needs to. Like Hawk said, fuck knows someone may as well make use of it," I said. "He doesn't care. Why do you sorry lot?"

Rollie was still grinning and Tank was doing a poor job of hiding a smile. Nico would have been smiling, no doubt, if he'd not been focussing on fifty things at once on his laptop as well as the conversation.

"It's just an interesting turn of events," Rollie said. "No more late night post-job parties. You'll have to actually wear clothes in your own damned house."

"I can't say I make a habit of walking around naked," I answered. I was too used to being ready for action that I was naked as little as possible.

Rollie's grin somehow got wider. "Why wear clothes when you don't have to?"

I huffed a laugh. "Yeah. I well remember, mate."

"Look, there are a lot of things that scarred me back there. But Rollie's naked arse has to be the worst," Hawk laughed.

Even as we all laughed with him – or smiled in my and

Nico's cases – we all knew that wasn't close to the truth. But sometimes the only way to give your demons less power over you was by telling yourself they already had no power over you.

"Fortescues?" I asked again.

"Go on, then," Nico said and that was our cue to move on.

Did it matter that I was the CEO of this company on paper? Did it matter that I was the unspoken leader of this merry band of misfits? Did it matter that I'd led them when we were back in special ops?

No.

Around this table, we weren't even equals. They all decided they were superior to me and Nico was somehow the one who called the shots.

Not that I cared really. We might not be shot at on an hourly basis anymore. We might not need months of hospital care and rehab after a job anymore. But our job was still stressful and any reprieve I could give my men would only mean that they worked better overall.

"Right. So Mrs Fortescue desires security for Friday. Can anyone fit her in?"

They all stared at me with barely concealed hostility, annoyance, or humour. I knew Rollie was one heartbeat away from a not entirely inaccurate inappropriate comment, but he was trying to decide how well his following argument was going to go down if he led with that.

Rollie opened his mouth, but Hawk beat him.

"I was hoping I could do Champers Day with Amber?" he said slowly, like it cost him some effort to admit that. Given that Rollie sniggered, it was probably not unwise on his part.

"Champers Day?" Tank asked before Rollie could shift his inappropriateness to Hawk's little sister.

Hawk shrugged. "She aced a major milestone in her thesis and she and that slag were supposed to celebrate. Except said slag was riding her boyfriend. I told Bert I'd celebrate with her as soon as I was free."

"We should all celebrate with her," Tank said evenly and we all looked at him. "Come on, we all know Farrah's going to side with Dannie."

And we were back to teenage gossip.

It was perhaps a fault of our many years of brotherhood that we knew so much about each other's lives. But when it was just ten of you in a tent for fuck knew how long with barely any electricity, let alone any other mode of entertainment – newbies learnt quick that wanking lost a lot of its appeal after weeks and with only nine other blokes for company – we ended up talking. Talk was inevitably about the people we missed at home, so we related our letters basically verbatim to each other to pass the time. It was our version of a soap opera.

"True, those bitches know nothing about loyalty," Nico added and we all turned to look at him in surprise.

"I've got a favour for Nelson on Friday, though," Rollie said.

"Saturday?" Hawk asked.

"I've got a…thing," Nico huffed.

Tank said, "I've got Falkner Saturday," but we were all focussed on Nico.

"What thing?"

"Like a date thing?" Rollie pressed. "Because I also have a date."

"No one's asking you about *your* date," Hawk told him as I said, "Leave O Lord alone."

"What about Sunday then?" Tank asked.

We all looked at each other – Rollie glaring at Nico's lack of information – and nodded.

"Okay," I said. "So, I'll deal with Mrs Fortescue on Friday. We'll do Champers Day on Sunday. And we're not going to bother O Lord about his…thing?" I looked down at the paper in front of me. "Mrs Fortescue only wants one of us until half ten, so that shouldn't be too hard."

There was silence as we all looked between each other. Eight years of knowing these guys and we could communicate with far more than words. When they all looked at me again – except Nico of course who was still busy behind his screen – I nodded.

"Right. Sorted." I stretched my neck and pulled my tie lose.

"Woohoo!" Rollie cried, pushing himself away from the table. "Meeting over."

"For me. Haven't you got to check on Jefferson this afternoon?" I looked at him and he sighed.

"Yes. I do." Rollie checked his watch. "Fuck. Now. May I be excused," he teased and I flicked my hand at him. He chuckled as he got up and swanned out yelling, "Nico, I need new comms. And I promise not to mention anything about *dates*!"

Nico's eyes stayed glued to his screen as he got up muttering to himself and followed Rollie out. I shared a smile with Hawk and Tank.

"Right. What have you boys got this afternoon?" I asked.

"Lesson with Mrs Hartley," Tank answered and we grimaced in sympathy.

"Have fun with that."

"Paperwork," Hawk sighed.

Tank snorted. "I think you win the shittest job competition," he said as he stood up.

"Ah, I dunno. Chaos has twice as much paperwork and I think he's got an issue with Falkner to deal with?"

"Oh, boss wins again!" Tank chuckled.

I stood up with a wry smirk. "And this is why I'm the boss."

"Oh. All work and no play make Chaos *vewy gwumpy*," Hawk teased.

I raised my eyebrow at him. "Chaos is always *vewy gwumpy*, birdboy," I replied deadpan and he and Tank barked laughter.

Hawk shook his head and I missed his words as I wandered to my office. We all had our own offices now, thank fuck. Back when we first started Grace Grayson

Security, Rollie was threatening to dismember the lot of us with far too much regularity and I was sure Nico had had the place bombed as insurance. Now we all had our own corners to have our personal time and things were a whole lot less tense.

Sometimes I wondered just how well we were all actually adjusting to civilian life again.

I sat at my desk and lost myself in my work for the rest of the day. Falkner was a fucking pain in the arse and no mistake. But when it came down to it, the man was scared of me. He put on a good face and his bluster got him so far. But when I put my foot down, he listened.

So it was after midnight by the time I'd dealt with all the bullshit behind the scenes things I'd never expected to have to deal with when Hawk and I drunkenly decided that we should go into private security; there was money in and out in every fucking direction, schedules, classes, copy for the website, and making sure Nico didn't get lost in the deep web and remembered to eat or sleep.

It seemed never ending. But it's not like I had anything else to focus my attention on. Still, I could only get by for so long telling the team to sleep if I didn't do it myself.

So I got up, grabbed my bag and wandered out. The rest of the guys had had jobs or classes all night, so they were gone. Except for one. The one who never left. I walked past his office on the way out and saw he was at least asleep. Sure, he was lying at what looked like a really awkward angle on his couch, his laptop on his legs and his glasses all wonky. But at least he wasn't still working.

I ducked in, closed his laptop and put it on his desk, slid his glasses off his face, threw a blanket over him, and turned out his light on my way out. Nico's and my SUVs were the only ones still in the parking garage and I couldn't say I was surprised; our building wasn't known for late-night businesses.

I was actually yawning by the time I pulled into my park in the Mayhew garage and I let out a deep breath before I dragged myself to the lift.

"Night, Mr Grayson," Nigel said too enthusiastically for the time of night.

"Night, Nigel."

"Anything exciting tonight?" he asked as I swiped my card.

"Just paperwork."

"Ah, damn."

Nigel had this idea that Grace Grayson Security were like superheroes or something. That we spent all night every night protecting hot young women from alien invaders or the Russian mob or something equally ridiculous. And look, sometimes that wasn't that far off base – not the aliens obviously – but our day-to-day was just driving people around and standing around while they did any number of fucking boring shit.

We were masters at blending into their world, but we didn't belong. We got by on our express ability to go unnoticed. And for Tank that wasn't as easily said as done;

the guy was almost seven feet tall and wide. He wasn't called Tank for nothing.

The lift doors finally slid open and I tried not to brush off Nigel's enthusiastic goodnight. I wasn't known for my friendliness, but I did try not to be an unmitigated arse.

I dropped my bag in my office and saw all the lights were on. I had a moment of panic as I heard rustling from the back. I stalked forward, my hand going to the holster under my jacket. And I was not expecting the sight that was waiting for me.

It wasn't a burglar. It wasn't some criminal assailant. It was my best friend's little sister's arse as she bent flat over the table and reached for something.

I froze, not sure what my mind was trying to think.

It was either going somewhere incredibly inappropriate as though she wasn't my best friend's little sister, or nowhere at all because she was my best friend's little sister, and it just couldn't seem to decide.

Amber was wearing tracksuit pants and one leg kicked like that was going to give her more reach. After a bit, she just lay down and groaned.

"I swear to all you hold holy, Geoffrey! Don't make me come over there," she muttered.

She pushed herself up from the table and huffed, and I dropped my hands to my side. As she turned, she caught sight of me, yelped and fell on her arse.

I blinked. "You okay?"

She scrambled up and pushed her glasses up her nose.

"Yep."

She was wearing another of those huge woollen jumpers, the sleeves so long she had to constantly keep pulling them up. Her hair was pulled back in a messy bun with wisps of hair escaping all over her head. Her glasses somehow managed to hide and magnify her eyes as she avoided looking at me.

Had she been any other woman in the world, I would have known what to do, what to say. I could have been witty, flirty, dismissive, possessive, professional, whatever the situation called for.

I could deal with flirty women. I could deal with intimidated women. I could deal with stunned and besotted women. I could deal with business women. But this indifference was something, even at thirty, I had no idea what to do with.

I'd never seen it in any other person but her and it caught me off guard.

The only thing I'd ever wanted was to at least get along with the most important person in my best mate's life. Amber meant more than the world to Hawk and I was nothing without Hawk. Our whole lives, I'd tried to work out how to get along with her for him and I just didn't know where to start.

"You find everything okay?" I asked, cursing my voice for coming across so emotionless and uncaring.

I was just tired and the way she confused me made me annoyed with myself.

She nodded again and looked almost everywhere but me. "Yep. All good. Uh, thanks for…all this…"

I nodded. "My pleasure. Do you need anything?"

She shook her head. "I'll pack this stuff up for you." She pointed behind her to the spread of papers and books that were taking up most of the dining table.

I had to say the mess was a surprise. I'd somehow not noticed it. If she needed that much spread, I wasn't surprised she wasn't in the second office. As much as mess made my skin crawl, I could live with some papers on the table if it made her life easier.

"No. It's fine. Make yourself comfortable." I undid another button on my shirt like that was going to diffuse my discomfort. "Did you make any progress?"

She shrugged. "Depends what you count as progress."

The tension was high between us, just like it always had been, as we stood silently for far too many minutes.

Now and then, her eyes slid to me, until she realised I was looking at her. Then she'd tuck her hair behind her ear or push up her glasses and look away again. She'd always been shifty around me, always awkward and uncomfortable. But this was a new level of uncomfortable I didn't remember seeing in her before.

She was hunched over and curled in on herself, like she was hiding.

She tucked hair unnecessarily behind her ear one last time and finally said, "Um, so. I slept until like five. So I'm not going to sleep anytime soon. But I can get out of the way if you'd prefer?"

I watched her carefully, wondering what was going through her head.

My training had made me watchful, always looking for motives and more than people wanted you to see. It had saved more than my team's lives more times than I cared to remember.

"No. You're fine. Like I said, make yourself at home. I want you to be comfortable."

She gave a small smile, but like she knew it was polite rather than that she was feeling it. "Thanks." She gave a weird nod. "I'll get back to it then… Stay out of your way…" she mumbled, pushed her glasses again and turned back to the table.

I had no idea how to assure her she wasn't in my way. All I was going to do was find something to eat and go to sleep. I had to be back at the office in something like seven hours anyway.

So instead of telling her she was in no way in my way, I shucked my jacket and dropped it over one of the bar stools. I grabbed a beer and some leftovers out of the fridge, chucked the food in the microwave and popped the top of the beer. I happened to look up and I saw Amber staring at me, her mouth dropped open in a perfect little 'o'.

Fuck me.

My thoughts tried their darnedest to veer towards highly inappropriate at a sight like that and I put a stop to it straight away. There was no way in hell I was allowed to think something like that about little Amber Grace. Not even if the Amber Grace in front of me was all woman now.

"Did you want one?" I asked her.

She shook her head and didn't close her mouth.

I raised my eyebrow at her as I took a sip. "You okay?"

She nodded. "You have a…"

I waited for her to continue, but she didn't. "You're going to need to be more specific."

"Gun," she hissed.

Fuck. "Uh, yeah. Sorry…" I put my hand to it self-consciously. "I usually get changed as soon as I get back. It's either out of here or locked up. So…you don't have to worry about it."

She nodded, still looking like she was about to run.

"Amber?"

"Yeah?" she breathed.

I think it was the longest time she'd ever looked at me. Or maybe the only time she'd ever actually, properly looked at me.

"I can lock it up at the office if you'd prefer?"

She shook her head again, seemed to get control of herself and looked down as she pushed her glasses up again. "No. No. It's fine." She waved a hand at me in what I assumed was supposed to be reassuring, but just felt dismissive. "I'm fine."

Something about the way she said that hit me. It was too much like a mantra. Too much like the way we laughed about Rollie's naked arse being the most scarring thing we'd seen together. Too much like she thought it would be true if only she said it enough.

The microwave beeped and my head was so deep in thought that I actually jumped at the sudden noise. My heart raced like I was back on a mission and we'd narrowly missed a bomb. But Amber's eyes were focussed on whatever was in front of her, her hand on her forehead and over her eyes like a shield, like she'd rather forget I was there.

I took a deep breath, shook myself out and went to lock up my gun.

As I went back out to eat and finish my beer, we didn't talk and the silence was deafening. My skin prickled as though her eyes were on me and there were scathing judgements on the tip of her tongue. I never knew why one of my greatest fears was the time I stopped assuming and finally *knew* that Amber hated me. But it played on me like nothing ever had before.

I didn't even put the TV on. The only noise in the house was the scratching of her pen, the clacking of her typing, or her shuffling papers. But it was oddly comforting. Knowing she was in the place, as hostile as it seemed to be, was a comfort and I felt myself relax a little even as I was tensing for a whole other reason.

3
Amber

I heard his door open and pulled my other book back to me.

"Did you forget something?" I asked, for a minute acting like I would with Patrick.

"What?"

I looked up at him then and saw he was in a completely different suit than I'd last seen him in. This one was dark blue with a white shirt, matching navy tie, and brown dress shoes. He was doing up cufflinks as he walked out of his room, giving me a funny look. And that did not distract from the fact that he was completely gorgeous. Him with his damned chiselled cheekbones, his perfect eyebrows, that strong jaw, those lips that barely ever rose and yet I'd still imagined what they'd feel like against me on far too many occasions.

"Did you not go to bed?" he asked, looking out the window like he just had to check that it was actually the next morning.

I followed his gaze and saw that the first hint of dawn was sneaking up the sky.

"Bugger," I muttered and looked at my page. "What time is it?"

"About half seven."

I nodded. "Great."

"So you haven't slept?" he asked, with his nonchalant ease.

"No, Kit," I huffed. "I haven't slept. I don't seem to do that anymore."

I took my glasses off and rubbed my eyes. Now he'd pulled me out of my research, I felt exhausted but my mind was wired. I knew if I went to bed then I'd just be lying there replaying everything. And Dannie and Brent were going to make a lot of appearances.

The day before, I'd showered and put away my clothes before I'd fallen onto the bed and slept like the dead for six hours. Then I'd dived into study. I ignored calls and messages from Dannie, Farrah and Brent – not that there were many – and I think I'd let my phone run out of batteries somewhere along the lines. Oh well, the only people who used it that I might have wanted to talk to were my parents and I didn't really want to talk to them just then anyway.

"Wi-Fi?" I heard myself say.

"What?" he asked.

I shook my head. "Do you have Wi-Fi?"

"Uh…" He paused and looked around. "Yeah, Nico set it up though. I'll get him to send you the…" He pulled his phone out of his pocket and held a hand up to me. I watched the corner of his lip quirk. Almost. "My bad, dude. But I need Wi-Fi–" He shook his head. "Get some coffee in you, will you? Amber needs the Wi-Fi details." Kit nodded. "Great. Thanks, man."

He hung up and looked at me. Which of course, meant I looked anywhere but at him.

"He's got a client to deal with but said he can drop past about lunchtime and set it up?" Kit said as he walked into the kitchen.

I nodded, sure I probably could have done it myself. But whatever worked for them. "Thanks."

"If you need it sooner–"

"No. I'm good. Just figured I'd need it at some point."

He nodded. "Coffee?"

I picked up my mug and wondered when I'd finished it. I opened my mouth to say thanks, but then realised that maybe I should hold off on the caffeine if I planned to sleep at all sometime that day. And I did need to sleep. But I also wanted to avoid my problems some more. Coffee it was.

I got up from the table and slid my mug across the counter to him. "Sure. Thanks."

I pulled myself onto his far too tall bar stools and watched him work, taking the time to let myself stare at him unashamedly. His jacket lifted and his suit pants pulled against his arse as he moved and I let myself appreciate it in a way that thirteen year old me and sixteen year old me hadn't really been able to do. Not that I remembered his arse being quite that tight.

God damn, but he made my knees weak and my

imagination run wild. I might not have experienced as much as other girls my age, but I'd read plenty of smutty romance before my thesis took over my life. So I could imagine with the best of them. In fact I was pretty sure Kit Grayson would make a stunning romance hero in a book one day – if I ever finished my thesis and had time to do non-uni-related things.

"Donald can let Nico in if you need to get some sleep," Kit said as he turned.

I freaked out so badly I slid off the stool.

I managed to get my feet under me in something that hopefully looked like I'd been intending to do it, rather than just falling over because this guy, so far out of my league, had a serious effect on me.

"Uh, sure. I don't know yet. I'll see how I go."

He nodded as he passed me my mug then stepped back and leant against the opposite counter. "Were you going to be around for dinner…? Or…?"

I snuck a look up at him. I don't think I'd ever seen Kit looked unsure and awkward before.

I'd seen him dark. I'd seen him brooding. I'd seen him smouldering. I'd seen him cheeky. I'd probably seen every side of the Chaos that there was. Except this one. This one was new. I wasn't so disillusioned by his amazing arse that I thought he was asking me out. He was obligated to make small talk. So, he was making small talk.

I pushed my glasses up and looked at my coffee. "I didn't have plans."

"Okay. Well, get anything up you want. They'll charge it to my account–"

I looked up at him quickly. "Oh, no. I couldn't–"

He nodded, that cheeky almost-smirk in place. "Yes, you could. Your brother loves telling me I have too much money. Consider this an investment. Anything you can charge to my account, do so."

I blinked at him. "Um…"

"Please, Amber. Hawk would want you taken care of while you're here."

"About that…?" I started.

He took a sip of his coffee and I wondered how you could drink coffee sexily. "What about it?"

"I'll look for another–" I stopped as he shook his head and pushed off the counter behind him.

"*Mi casa es tu casa.* As long as you want. How much longer have you got on your degree?"

"Uh, something like three years minimum…?"

He shrugged. "Three years minimum, then. I'm not just bragging when I say I can afford it, Amber." His eyes twinkled far too enticingly, something primal in there, but I was pretty sure he wasn't doing it on purpose. "But it would also be my pleasure. Anything that can make your life easier, I'd be happy to give you. No expectations, just a favour to Hawk and you."

What would make my life easier was for him to be less sexy. Was for him to stop popping up in my deepest, darkest, most debased fantasies where he did things to me I don't think I'd ever let anyone to do me in real life. But I couldn't say any of that. And Kit was being serious anyway.

Thirty-year-old Kit wasn't like twenty-two-year-old Kit. I mean, he was. But there was this weird adult vibe about him I was pretty sure I'd never find. He legitimately cared about his best friend's little sister and I had to appreciate that as much as I appreciated his arse. And to be honest, any amount of not having to look after myself would be great. I was on a two week sabbatical from work, and I wasn't looking forward to going back. If I lived with Kit until I finished my thesis, then I wouldn't have to work and I could actually focus on study. I could sleep without worry that I was wasting precious time off.

"Thanks. That would be…" I forced myself to look up at him, but it only lasted a second. "That would be amazing. Thank you."

"Sister of my brother," he said again.

"What does that mean?" I asked quickly before I lost my nerve.

He looked me over casually, like he was trying to construct his answer properly. "Hawk's like a brother to me, my life is nothing without him in it. You're not just his actual sister, but his favourite person in the whole fucking world. So like I'd do anything for him, I'd do anything for you."

"Anything," I couldn't stop myself saying.

He nodded, no bluster, no joke, all serious. "Anything." His eyes slid behind me to the window.

I decided not to go near the whole sexual implication I could go with there. "You'd die for me?" But bordering on sassy was apparently still within the parameters. I was so proud of myself.

The corner of his lip twitched and then he smiled as his nose twitched like he was trying to stop it. "Yeah. I'd die for the both of you. No questions. Fuck," he huffed as he ran his hand through his hair, "I almost died for Hawk plenty of times."

Something twisted in my gut as I watched him. Then he looked back to me and I looked away again.

"It's not quite as dramatic as it sounds."

My eyes snapped up with a question.

"That I'd die for you. Spending years putting your life on the line for other people." He shrugged. "It becomes second nature after a while."

"Oh." I wasn't going to pretend to myself that I hadn't hoped it was just as dramatic as it sounded. "No. Of course." I cleared my throat and turned away to the table.

I started shuffling papers on the table like I had a purpose.

I had no right to even want more from Kit. I'd never had that right. He was my older brother's best friend, he was dark and dangerous, and he'd been damaged long before he went away. I was nothing and no one to forget for any length of time that I'd be anything other than a favour for Patrick.

I was the nothing and no one who had just walked in on her boyfriend under her best friend only the morning before because she was the freak who was still a virgin at twenty-three. Even if I somehow found myself in any zone remotely sexy and one that wouldn't bring down the wrath of my older brother, Kit wouldn't want a twenty-three-year-old virgin. He wouldn't want a girl who couldn't keep a guy for longer than a few months. I'd been geeky and nerdy enough before he'd left; I was ten times worse now.

Every woman I'd ever seen Kit with was tall, leggy, exotic, stunning, with a dirty streak that matched his own. I didn't think I could summon tall, leggy, exotic, stunning, or dirty if I had the Idiot's Guide and a life-time of practise. Let alone the whole combination.

"Okay. I'll leave you to…whatever it is you do…" Kit said, just cementing in my mind that this whole book geek thing was never going to be sexy for him.

I nodded. "Sure. Secure good and all that."

I heard him make a noise and turned to see a faint smile on his face. "Yeah. I'll do that."

I gave him a small smile that for once didn't feel like I had to force it because it was expected. "Bye."

"I'll see you later, Amber," he said with a nod.

I snuck a look at him as he walked out and breathed out heavily.

"God," I breathed. "This is simultaneously the worst idea and the best idea you've ever had."

It was going to be fine as long as I remembered he was out of my league. If that didn't work, I'd remind myself he was off-limits. If that didn't work, I'd go take a look in the mirror and remember why he'd never be interested. And if that failed, then I'd just be my usual level of weird and awkward around him.

"Yeah, that'll work," I told myself as I sat down and went back to my research.

I must have once again got lost in it, because the next thing I knew I heard an unfamiliar voice.

"Ah. Hi…"

I looked up from my papers and my breath hitched. "Hi…" came out as some choked breath.

In front of me was the dorky geek of your dreams. He was thin and lean, but probably almost as tall as Patrick, not as tall as Kit. He wore glasses and his scruffy blond hair fell into his eyes. He wore a totally geeky t-shirt under his undone hoody that made the geek in me squeal in excitement, and tan chinos with red Converses. He had a satchel slung over his shoulder and rubbed his arm as I looked at him.

"Amber, yeah?" he asked.

I nodded. "Um. Yeah. Nico, I assume?"

He nodded. "Yep. I hear you need Wi-Fi."

"I do. Thanks."

He gave another awkward nod and took a step forward. My phone was charging in the kitchen and it chose that moment to go off. Nico looked at me suspiciously for a moment, pointing over his shoulder back to where my phone was with a question on his face. Yeah, it was the Doctor's TARDIS materialising…

I nodded and bit my lip against a smile. "Guilty." I pointed at his shirt, where a Storm Trooper was looking at a line-up of a whole lot of robots from different fandoms; Bender, a dalek, R2D2, C-3PO, even Wall-E was there. "I love your shirt."

He grinned widely before he looked down at it and holy hells the guy was hot. "Thanks. Chaos got it for me last Christmas." He looked back up at me and I knew I hadn't been imagining things.

Nerd boy was hot. Not Kit-level hot. But he had the addition of that geeky charm that I could totally relate to.

"Did he have any idea what it meant?" I asked, fighting a smile.

Nico shook his head. "No fucking clue."

I snorted. "Why am I not surprised."

"What do you need set up?" he asked.

"Uh, laptop and phone I think?"

"E-reader? Tablet?"

I nodded. "Good thinking. I'll grab them."

He grinned and I decided I liked Nico; he was someone I knew how to deal with. Geek I spoke. "I'll get started on your laptop?"

I nodded as I hurried off to my room to grab my e-reader, after a few minutes of hunting around for it and finding it had fallen under the bed. By the time I got back, Nico was looking over my spectacular mess on the table. He flicked his eyes up to me and pointed at it.

"This shit is heavy," he whistled.

Here was a guy who obviously appreciated the geek in a woman.

He is also off-limits, I reminded myself.

Nico hadn't trained with the others – he'd been a replacement tech guy, fifty points to the house of your choice if you can work out what happened to the first guy – but he'd become just as close with Patrick as Kit was. Older brother's mates were off-limits. It was like an unspoken rule. Unless you were in a trashy romance and then you could have whoever the hell you wanted.

I brushed my hair back. "Yeah. It's…like quicksand. One step in and I'm deep."

He chuckled. "I get it."

I looked up at him. "Yeah?"

"Yeah." He nodded. "I've lost count of the times Chaos has to literally pull me off the computer to sleep or eat. I get sucked into a whole new world."

I smiled at him. "Me too."

I passed him the e-reader and he did whatever he needed to do, his long fingers flying nimbly over the screen much faster than mine ever could. It was damned mesmerising. Finally he passed it back with a smile.

"I'd best get back. Tank vowed to wipe the floor with me in our sparring session and I should be suitably wary."

I knew enough about the boys to remember their codenames better than their first names, even if I hadn't met them. "He's likely to?"

Nico snorted. "Tank would wipe the floor with The

Rock."

I breathed out. "Ah."

"Yeah. But we have mandatory sparring. Chaos doesn't want us going soft."

"Sensible."

Nico crooked his eyebrow at me. "I live behind a screen. I haven't needed combat in…fuck, years."

"And when the baddies break into your office?"

"Then I'll tell them I'm not the droids they're looking for and hopefully distract them for long enough that Chaos or Hawk can come and kick some arse."

I sniggered. "Sounds like a legit strategy."

"Much, you'll find, like camping," he quipped as though it was second nature, but I knew what he was referring to.

"Ah, no. I think you'll find that immoral."

He looked at me like he wondered where I'd come from. "What would you know about it?"

"I know that a spawn point is sacred, dude. Don't desecrate the spawn point."

"Fuck," he chuckled, twisting like he was going to walk away. "Hawk never said you were cool."

I laughed. "That's probably because he doesn't think I am."

Nico waved a hand at me. "Wanker's not all that." He checked his watch and swore again. "I've gotta cruise. Aces to meet you. I'll see you later, I hope?"

I nodded. "I hope so."

He grinned, gave me a nod, and hurried out.

See, I could talk to men. They just had to be my own kind.

I checked my phone and found it had enough battery for me to call my boss and quit. I wasn't looking forward to it, but he knew how stressed I'd been with my thesis so he'd understand.

I hoped.

4

Kit

When I walked in at around three, Amber was sucking on a pen and I had a very traitorous moment.

"Hey," I said.

She looked up and there was a flash of something that passed over her face. I was almost convinced her eyes had widened and she'd caught her lip in her teeth at the sight of me. I told myself it wasn't there. I'd seen nothing. It couldn't have been there. Especially because a moment later she was avoiding looking at me again. And her tone was totally nonchalant.

"Hey. You finish early?"

I shook my head. "Need to change for a job. I'll be out late."

She nodded. "Okay."

"You're…okay?" I asked.

She nodded again. "All good. Thanks."

Not knowing what else to say, I went to my room to change and hurried back out again as soon as possible.

"I'll see you tomorrow, then."

52

"Sure. Bye," she replied with an absent wave as she looked over one of her books.

I sighed and headed back down to my SUV, feeling antsy and uncomfortable.

I was meeting the boys at an event – one of the many galas the Nelsons put on for charity – and was in danger of being pretty well on time now. But that made for a nice change.

When I got out and headed for the foyer of the theatre, I saw that Tank was already there and Rollie was pretending to throw punches at him. Nico and Hawk were having an in-depth discussion, arms pointing in different directions, as Nico looked at his tablet.

"Going over the layout?" I asked as I walked up to them.

Hawk nodded. "One final sweep. Everything looks good."

"I don't know why I had to be on the ground for this," Nico grumbled.

"Because the Nelsons have zero faith in their tech skills," Hawk answered.

"Did you get to the penthouse?" I asked Nico.

Nico actually looked up from his tablet and had a vague hint of a smile on his face. "Oh, yeah. Hey." He nudged his elbow towards Hawk. "You never told us your sister was cool."

Hawk stopped his survey and turned to Nico in surprise. "Cool?" he scoffed. "Bert's not cool."

Nico gave Hawk a look that suggested he very much

disagreed. "Hate to be the bearer of bad news, dude. But your sister's definitely cool."

I was obviously not the only one who heard the appreciation in his voice.

Hawk pointed at Nico. "Just what do you mean by she's cool?"

Nico shrugged. "I mean she's cool, man. She's great."

Hawk was obviously not sure how to take the news, and I wasn't sure how I felt about it either. Nico's eyes lit up at the thought of Amber. What did that mean? Nico's eyes were known to light up at the thought of pizza, so it didn't have to mean he was interested in her. But was he?

"Great how?" Hawk asked, his eyes narrowing in suspicion.

"She speaks my language, for one thing. Obviously games. Into the same shit as me. Knows about than sanctity of the spawn point."

I'd heard about the sanctity of the spawn point. I still had no idea what it meant. I felt a momentary twinge of something too akin to jealousy that Nico had met her once and had already managed a better conversation than I had with her in twenty-three years.

Hawk looked at me. "She might come in handy for this year's Christmas presents."

"She did get my t-shirt," Nico said proudly.

I remembered which one he'd been wearing that morning. It was the one I'd bought him last Christmas. I hadn't understood the reference, but the guy at the comic book store assured me it would go down well.

"It's not like he has the most obscure taste on the planet," I huffed, straightening my jacket unnecessarily and looking around like I was doing another sweep.

"Yeah, but I might actually win the present contest this year with Bert's help."

"I would be very interested to see what she'd come up with for me," Nico said and the appreciation was well obvious in his voice this time.

"Just you watch how interested in my sister you are there, Nico," Hawk warned.

Nico actually laughed, and it was almost self-conscious, both of which were odd for him and made me doubt his next words. "I'm not interested in your sister. I just think she's cool." He paused, then added, "She's probably the coolest chick I've met."

"You touch her and you're dead," I growled.

Hawk's mouth had been open to say something, his finger pointing at Nico again. But at my words, he turned to me, still pointing at Nico, and blinked a couple of times. He finally shut his mouth, looked at Nico, back to me, another couple of blinks, then back at Nico.

"Yeah," he finally said, far less threateningly after my outburst. "What he said. Bert's off-limits, mate."

"Who's fucking Amber?" Rollie asked as he and Tank strolled over.

"No one," Hawk and I snapped at the same time.

Rollie held his hands up, his trademark smirk on his face.

"All right. Slow your rolls, gentleman. I was just interested in why Hawk's giving us the 'off-limits' speech now."

"What is that supposed to mean?"

Rollie rocked back on his heels, his smirk growing. "Well, only that you've known us for fucking years and not once has this been mentioned. We talk about her all the time. Fuck, I feel like I already know her. But not once have you felt the need to tell us not to go near her."

"One could extrapolate either you're worried about us finally meeting her on Sunday, or Chaos has been misbehaving—"

"I've done nothing of the sort!" I said too loudly, as the same time Hawk said, "He knows better than that."

Hawk kicked his chin to Nico. "This muppet on the other hand."

Tank looked at me, eyebrow cocked in question and I cleared my throat. "Our resident nerd seems to think Amber's...cool," I said.

Nico's cheeks got a touch of pink to them. "Yeah. I said she was cool. What's wrong with her being cool?"

There was a lot wrong with him thinking she was cool. But I'd already had two too many outbursts in the last few minutes concerning her, so I bit my cheek to stop myself saying anything. Rollie had no such qualms.

Rollie grinned. "Oh, the O-Lord wants to give her a private lesson in..." he petered off and frowned.

"Yeah, I was wondering where that was going," Hawk sniggered. "Dipshit thinks he knows everything about tech."

"I know more than you!"

"Ah, Mr Grayson and company," came a voice to put a stop to our ridiculous bickering.

I turned on my polished heel and nodded to our client, thankful to get everyone's minds on work.

"Mr Nelson, thank you for trusting us with your safety."

He waved a hand at me and smiled. "Oh, five big, strapping men? You have my utmost trust, boys."

Rollie smiled. "We aim to please, sir."

Mr Nelson smirked knowingly. "So, I've heard. Just don't remind my husband. Now, the guests are set to arrive from five…"

The rest of my night was as boring as usual. Keep an eye on things. Be the relay man between Mr Nelson out in the party and the behind the scenes people. Be stern and foreboding so the guests knew there was a security presence – Mr Nelson liked us to be obvious, to be visible. He said it made him feel more important because none of his friends ever had any reason to justify hiring security, although how much of that was a joke I never quite knew as most of his friends had hired one or more of us at some point. He was one of our more generous clients though, so we bent over backwards to accommodate him. He was also just a nice guy.

Tank pulled off visible with ease by his sheer size alone. Hawk and Rollie were also excellent at making sure people knew they were around and very intimidating, as well as cheeky when anyone even vaguely flirted with them.

Thankfully Nico was hidden away behind computer screens most of the night as he was the least foreboding of the lot of us and the one with the least patience for jobs that required acting a part other than just nondescript security.

Finally, the last guests left and Mr Nelson dismissed us for the night. Nico ripped his tie off at the first possible opportunity, while the rest of us just loosened them a little. We said goodnight, and the boys and I went in our own directions.

I dropped my bag in my office as I pulled off my jacket and ran my hand over my hair. There was something about messing it up at the end of the day that made it really feel like the end of the day. I headed for my bedroom to change, trying to remember if I had any leftovers in the fridge when I realised I smelled something familiar. It was mild, merely a lingering scent, but it made me think of family dinners and laughter.

It was definitely vague and I was acclimatising to it by the second, but it was there. I just couldn't work out what it was.

Suddenly, adrenalin surged and I was ready for whatever it was as my eyes scanned the penthouse. I was just about to spring into action when I realised that the slumped figure at the dining table was Amber.

"Don't live alone anymore," I muttered, looking around. That was the second night in a row I'd forgotten.

The lights were all off so she must have been asleep for hours.

"Fuck, that can't be comfortable."

I threw my jacket over one of the other chairs and went over to her. I crouched down, but she was fast asleep. Her books and papers were still all over the table, her laptop sitting dead by her elbow. I stood and leant over to look at it all by the moonlight streaming into the room. I caught mentions of round tables and wizards and epic battles, but I'd lost my decent night vision from a lack of use over the last couple of years.

"Amber?" I said softly.

She moved a little, but made no sign she was going to wake up.

For the second night in a row, I slid the sleeper's glasses off their face. This time though, I gently picked her up. She didn't wake, but she snuggled into me and I'm man enough to admit that I had a moment where I saw my entire life being different. I did, however, try not to look too closely at it.

I carried her effortlessly to bed, catching a lingering floral scent in her hair. For the second time in as many minutes, something felt familiar, but I couldn't work out where from. But it made me think of summer days in the Graces' backyard, it made me think of late night movies on the back wall and popcorn fights, it made me think of good times and happiness.

Before I set her on her bed, I looked down at her. I couldn't remember ever seeing her asleep. But she looked peaceful. There was no sign of the anger or annoyance or whatever it was that she felt when I was around. I could almost imagine what it would have been like if we'd got along, if she looked up to me the same way she looked up to Hawk.

Something fiercely protective reared up in me and I wondered how in the hell anyone could hurt her. I completely agreed with Hawk's assessment; I ever saw the fucker, then I was going to drag him to the deepest, darkest hole on the planet. And I was pretty sure I knew exactly which hole Hawk was thinking of. And I thought it was probably the best choice. That went for Dannie, too. Dannie, who had never once put Amber first, was just as much to blame.

Amber wriggled against me and I panicked she was going to wake up and freak out. Honestly I wouldn't have blamed her. This would look weird.

I lay her down on the bed and watched as she did that little nose wrinkle she did. She had a million of them. But this one I couldn't quite place. It was like she'd heard Hawk tell a dirty joke she found funny but didn't think she should. But it also looked like one I hadn't seen before. I wondered what she was dreaming of.

I put her glasses on the bedside table and pulled the other half of the blankets over her before I went over and closed the curtains. The soldier in me did a final scan of the room – still as bare as it had been the day before – and looked back at her once more.

I closed the door and headed out to get changed and find

some dinner.

Carmel was going to kill me with her tiny little bare hands if she found out I'd skipped on dinner again. She was already complaining I was getting too skinny. No amount of assuring her I was putting on weight made her feel any better.

Once my suit was hung and I'd thrown on a pair of track pants, I headed for the fridge. There was a container there that I was sure hadn't been there that morning. I pulled it out and found a chicken casserole. I knew for a fact that the restaurant didn't make that chicken casserole and one whiff confirmed it was the recipe I'd shovelled by the plate-load for years at the Graces'. It was the smell that had been lingering when I entered, obviously from when she'd eaten, possibly not that long ago. I wondered if Hawk had found his way over after all.

I warmed some up and ate it as I looked over the counter to the table. Usually I was a neat freak – ironic given my nickname, I know, but less ironic given my years of military life. It was a weirdly neat mess, anyway. A mess that looked useful, necessary. A mess I could abide. And there was something oddly pleasant about evidence another human being was there with me.

Even if it was just my best friend's little sister. Even if I barely saw her. Even if we barely spoke to each other. Even if she hated me. I realised it had been lonely in that big place all by myself for so long. And no matter how awkward I got around her indifference, it was going to be nice to not be alone anymore.

5
Amber

I sat bolt upright, expecting a crick in my neck. Then I registered that my vision was fuzzy. Then I registered I'd been lying down.

I looked down, thinking I must have fallen off my chair in the middle of the night – wouldn't have been the first time. But that was definitely a bed under me. And I was still wearing my shoes. I blinked as I looked around the practically lightless room. There was only the faintest hint of sun coming around the curtains and it was wan. I looked over and saw my glasses were on the bedside table. I picked them up suspiciously as I looked around and suddenly wondered where I was.

I slowly slid on my glasses and suddenly everything came flooding back.

Dannie and Brent.

Patrick and Kit.

Nico and the droids.

Studying at the dining table all day because I couldn't bring myself to go to sleep. Again.

"Wait..."

I looked around again.

I had absolutely no memory of going to bed. And there was the weird thing about still wearing my shoes and I was on top of the sheets under half a blanket. My cheeks flushed moments before I realised that all these things were adding up to the presumption that I'd fallen asleep at the table and Kit had brought me to bed when he got home.

"Oh, nice work, goober," I muttered as I pulled myself out of the blanket and tried to remember what I'd shoved in the great Suitcase of Leaving that could be classified as clothes.

I pulled off yet another oversized jumper and dropped it on the bed as I stretched my slightly stiff neck and kicked off my shoes. I rifled through drawers and the (massive and almost empty) walk in robe for something to wear.

"Why did I pack so much underwear?" I muttered to myself.

And it wasn't the everyday kind. I'd apparently just scooped out my entire lingerie collection – all those racy things that Dannie, Farrah and I loved buying but I'd had absolutely no reason to wear and now had no one to wear it for – without thinking of what I was actually going to wear. On closer inspection, it seemed like I'd done that for most of my clothes. It was lucky it was winter and most of my drawers had consisted of pants and jumpers.

Given the spectacular amount of nothing that really went together, I settled on some jeans and a hoody. I did a quick pass through the bathroom to detangle my hair and regain some sense of humanity before I wandered out to the main room. I always found that humanity made for a pretty decent start to the day.

Coffee also made a very good start to the day and it was all I could smell as I walked out of the little side passage and my stomach rumbled angrily.

"God, how long did I sleep?" I asked myself as I headed for the kitchen.

Kit kept saying make myself at home, so I guess I was going to do just that.

Halfway to the kitchen, I was stopped in my tracks as Kit walked out of his bedroom in nothing but his suit pants as he ran a hand over his hair. And blow me down. My knees nearly buckled out from under me where I stood.

Muscles bulged and rippled where they quite frankly had no place being. He had tattoos covering his left shoulder and down to his elbow, one on his right pec, and something on his right rib. And that had nothing on the scars I could see even from that distance. Not that they did anything but add to the sinfully sexy damaged bad boy persona Kit had exuded since his early teens.

And just as I was gawking, he pulled his eyes from the window and saw me. His step faltered. I wasn't sure if he was surprised to see me, just being wary around me, or had noticed the drool I suspected was hanging out of my mouth.

"Morning…" he said slowly.

His eyes took me in quickly, no doubt from years of

having to read a room for any immediate danger. As he did, his expression turned almost cheeky like he knew exactly what was going through my head. I was suddenly super certain he could see every single dirty thought I'd ever had of him. I looked at him just long enough to half-wonder if that excited him.

The nerves won out and I did that super wanky thing where I pushed my glasses up my nose as I averted my gaze and nodded. "Morning."

"Coffee?" he asked and I wondered if I'd just imagined a whole exchange between us.

"I can…" I started, gave up, then hurried over to the machine.

It seemed no amount of small talk one day prepared me for the next time I saw him. Each time, it was like I was back at square one trying to not be a dick so hard that I was an even bigger dick. It wasn't surprising he was wary around me; I probably came across as idiotic bitch incarnate.

The hairs on the back of my neck were standing up and I snuck a look over my shoulder to see him leaning his hip against the other side of the counter, his arms crossed over that beautiful body, and watching me intently, like he knew something. As usually awkward as usual, I focussed on what I was doing and didn't let his scrutiny get to me.

What had I expected if I was going to be living in his house? Of course there'd be awkward mornings and him taking me to bed and the need to talk to each other and me being a complete and utter tool. I was probably just lucky we hadn't had more of it yet.

"Amber…" he started and I actually jumped in surprise.

"Yeah?" I squeaked, cleared my throat and tried again. "Yep?"

"I just want you to know that you *are* welcome here. I'm happy to have you here. You're not getting in my way and you can just be yourself."

I nodded, having no idea what that tone of voice was supposed to be. It wasn't quite the tone you use on frightened animals, but it was close. Imagine trying to get a wary dog to trust you but finding it amusing at the same time. That was what Kit's voice sounded like.

"Thanks. I'm—"

I spluttered as I moved the damn milk jug the wrong way and it spat hot milk all over me. And of course, I dropped the jug on the floor for good measure, throwing hot milk all down my jeans' leg. I stood in the middle of the floor, refusing to look at him while I took a deep breath. Out of pure instinct, I held up a hand to let him know that comments were not welcome. That move wouldn't have stopped Patrick.

"Paper towel?" I asked slowly.

"What?" he asked.

"Tea towel?" I tried.

"Oh, right. Here."

I turned to see whether my peripheral vision had actually been playing tricks on me. But no. Kit had just slid himself effortlessly over the top of the kitchen counter, dropped to a crouch, and was now getting a tea towel out of one of the drawers.

When he stood, we were standing very close together and I took the tea towel he proffered with one hand while I pushed on my glasses with the other – *stop that!* Our fingers brushed and my heart fluttered wildly. It wasn't just nervousness, it was more. It was electrifying. My years of reading trashy romance novels gave me plenty of fodder for my imagination, but I could *not* think of Kit like that.

"Thanks," I said, hoping I didn't sound as breathless as I felt.

When he said nothing, my eyes darted up and I saw the humour in his and the smirk that played at his lips. We were both still holding onto the tea towel, our knuckles touching through the flimsy material. My heart floundered hard in my chest as we looked at each other and I imagined a moment – half a moment – where he wasn't my brother's best friend and I could just openly ogle him to my heart's content. And for even less of a moment, I let myself imagine the look in his eyes meant he felt the same way.

But my eyes fell as they usually did whenever I actually looked at him and I was partially distracted as they came to a rest on the tattoo on his pec. It was a sword surrounded by stars and…maybe like rays of light?

"Our unit…got them together when our first commander died," Kit said, his voice heavy.

My eyes flicked up for a moment, then got a stark

reminder of why we don't look at him full on and they dropped again. They fell on his right rib and I felt myself smile.

"How fitting," I muttered.

"What?" he asked.

I couldn't have stopped my fingers trailing over the Latin words if I'd wanted to. "'By the grace of chaos'," I translated softly and this time when I looked up his eyes were soft and I felt like he was answering my unbidden smile.

Warmth rose up in my chest as we just stood looking at each other. My heart beat a little faster and a whole slew of unlikely futures rushed through my mind unbidden. God, he was attractive and that slightly cocky hint of humour in the corner of his lips did other things to my insides that I both loved and hated.

Something swirled around us, warm and expectant. It was tense, but a delicious kind of tense. He licked his lip and, for the space of another heartbeat, the ridiculous idea hit me that he might kiss me. I was pretty sure I'd risk Patrick's wrath for one taste. History be damned, I'd die happy for one single taste.

I felt my lips part slightly. Kit's eyes dropped to them for a split-second. I inhaled sharply…

Then it was like I could suddenly only just feel the heat of his skin under my finger tips and I consciously realised I was touching him. Actually freaking touching Kit Grayson. Not just a slight accidental brushing of skin, but like full on touching. And no one was putting a stop to it. Someone had to put a stop to it before I did something stupid.

I pulled my hand back slowly.

"Sorry," I said quickly as I turned to deal with the milk in the hopes he wouldn't see if that heat in my cheeks had sent them pink.

"Don't be." He seemed to clear his throat. When he spoke again, it felt like he was trying to change the subject. "I assumed Hawk had shown you."

Happy not to dwell, I shook my head as I pulled off my glasses to wipe them clean enough for now.

"I thought you caught up at Christmas?" he asked.

I nodded, then couldn't help looking back at him with a slight smile. "How often do you think I see Pat naked?"

Surprised flitted across his features as he gave me a crooked smile, but his eyes had this look like the action was foreign to him now. "I'm hardly naked."

"True." I nodded, sort of very much wishing he was. "But no. I haven't seen Pat without his shirt on probably since before you left. Alas, our schedules just haven't lined up."

He snorted. "You don't go home a lot."

I went home plenty. I just managed to only go home when Patrick wasn't likely to feel the need to remove clothing. Even when I hung out at his, he always wore at least a singlet.

"Neither do you," I reminded him.

There was a pause, but for once I didn't feel awkward.

Well not completely awkward. Only what seemed like a reasonable level of awkwardness after you've just thrown milk all over yourself.

"You know, I think this is the longest conversation we've ever had," he mused.

I looked back at him again and saw him leaning against the bench with that cocky smirk. A zing of something shot through me and I had trouble keeping my own smirk off my face.

"I think you're right," I replied, going back to my milk problem.

Suddenly, there was a string of angry sounding…maybe Spanish – dead languages, I'm your girl, live ones…not so much – and a masculine yelp. I spun quickly, slipped on a patch of milk and my legs went out from under me with a yelp of my own.

The tiny little woman standing in the opening to the kitchen smacked Kit again and snapped at him, to which he replied in perfect…whatever it was. *God, I have to get better at this stuff…*

"Okay, okay," Kit said, waving his hands at her. He stepped towards me and held his hands out.

Under the glare of the angry woman, I didn't hesitate to take them and let him help me up. Oh, more touching. My heart fluttered, but the presence of a third person had me keeping my head. Sort of.

"Are you okay?" he asked, his eyes staring super intensely right into mine and literally taking my breath away.

Reminding myself I was the only one hung up in a moment, I nodded and took my hands back as quickly as wouldn't seem rude. The damn things tingled at his touch and I was having trouble breathing. I subconsciously wiped my hands on my pants, feeling like they were suddenly super sweaty and gross. All the awkwardness was back.

Kit cleared his throat and stepped back. "Carmel, this is Amber."

Carmel took her glare off Kit and gave me a warm smile. "Miss Amber, lovely to meet you. When Christopher told me he had a young lady living with him, I got all excited. Then the great lummox is standing around while you clean up. You were brought up better than that, *mijo*. I'm disgusted in you."

Kit replied to her in Spanish with a frown.

"So?" she asked, throwing me a look I felt like I was supposed to know about. "I don't care if she's your maid or the woman who'll bear your children. You show her some damned respect!"

Kit looked at me in the same sort of cheeky way he'd have looked at Patrick in that moment and Carmel smacked him upside the head. I covered my mouth just not quickly enough to hide my laugh. I saw Kit's eyebrows rise at me as a smile played at his lips. It might not have been sexual tension, but it was definitely the height of Chaos cheek and that was just as dangerous.

Carmel frowned at him again, then turned to me and took

my hands.

"Anything you need, *mija*, you let me know. Shopping list, washing, dry cleaning," she threw a pointed look to Kit, "man trouble. I'm here. My numbers and things are in the book in the top drawer in the table in the hall. I've got used to Christopher's odd hours and he pays me handsomely for any bother." She winked. "So feel free to bother me whenever you like." She looked me up and down. "Oh you are beautiful, aren't you? Nothing like that lummox of a brother of yours."

I giggled, my nose wrinkling the way it did. "Thank you," I placated her.

But she seemed to know I disagreed. "You don't think so?" She made a tutting noise. "Shame. We'll have to find a real man to prove it to you." Here, she winked again.

I blushed so hard I was sure I went pink this time and I fiddled with my glasses again and I choked on my own spit. "Uh, I think I'm okay. Thanks, though."

Kit said something in Spanish and Carmel's eyes softened as she nodded. "The boys will look after you, *mija*. They're a boisterous lot, but their hearts are in the right place."

I nodded to her. "You might be right."

She smiled. "Now…" She turned back to Kit. "Why are you half naked when there are young ladies in the house?"

Kit looked suitably chastened. "I left my clean shirt in the hallway and then there was the milk mishap."

"Yes. That you didn't do anything about."

I smiled as I watched them banter, slipping between Spanish and English. I'd had no idea Kit knew Spanish. I wondered if maybe he'd learnt on a mission. I wondered if that meant Patrick knew Spanish too.

The milk on my jeans was getting cold.

I'd have to interrupt them to get past them to go and get changed. I waved my hand stupidly like I was still in class and cleared my throat. "Uh…"

Kit's eyes flew to me, and Carmel turned.

"Sorry. I should go change my…" I hung my head and grimaced as I realised I was swiftly running out of wearable clothes.

"What is it?" Carmel asked.

I forced a smile. "Nothing. It's fine. I'm fine."

Carmel frowned just like my mum would if I'd tried to lie to her and I felt the truth coming out. Well, the semi-truth.

"I'm just going to need to wash earlier than planned."

The full truth would be that I needed to go and face my ex-best friend and potentially my ex-boyfriend to pack up the rest of my stuff. And move it…into Kit's place, I guessed.

Carmel's frown brightened. "Leave it in your hamper and I'll sort it tomorrow."

"I can do it—"

"Where? The great lummox doesn't have a laundry. No. It's fine. It's what he pays me for. I'll pick it up tomorrow." She looked over Kit. "I suppose you'll need shirts doing?"

73

He nodded. "Thanks. We had a couple of…other mishaps this week."

She snapped at him in Spanish and he coyly shrugged as he replied. There was something adorable in the way he was letting himself be chastened by this fierce little woman.

Carmel gave me that look again like she'd strangle him if he wasn't a favourite and shook her head. "Honestly, how hard is it to put bloody clothes in the sink? Blood stains you know." She threw her arm up and muttered some more as she wandered out of the kitchen.

We both watched her until she'd disappeared into Kit's room.

"So…" I started. "She's fun."

Kit huffed a laugh. "Yeah. Carmel's good people. She's not joking, by the way. Anything you need, whenever you need it. She'll do it."

"Shopping, though?"

He nodded. "Yeah, she keeps me stocked. She says I give her something to do during the day, so she won't hear of you shopping."

"I suppose the money is a nice incentive."

He ran his hand through his hair and huffed self-consciously. With a shirt on, the action was distracting. Without a shirt, I felt in need of a cold shower.

"Yeah. I got lucky. And that means I can compensate my staff accordingly."

"If only Principal Whethers could see you now," I mused mock-wistfully.

And I made a mental note not to try to make jokes around him again.

He broke out into the most gorgeous full smile and those rich brown eyes sparkled. It did all sorts of funny things to my stomach that I'd hoped I'd grown out of, but had realised only moments ago I definitely had not. It wasn't just the 'jump me now' things, it was the ridiculous giggle things, it was the heart beating erratically things, it was the shallow breath things. It was all the things.

"Yeah," he laughed. "That would be sweet. Shame I missed the reunion."

"I've got my five year later this year, I could catch him up?" popped out of my mouth without licence as I seemed to have forgotten I was talking to Kit not Patrick.

That smile widened and I had to force myself to breathe. "Sure, sounds good."

Carmel appeared, muttering in Spanish again. Kit gave me that rueful smirk and went over to her. I, meanwhile, hurried off to my room to get changed and cool down after the force of that smile.

"You are in so much trouble, Amber," I told myself as I pulled on my tracksuit pants.

How was I supposed to live with a guy who turned my brain to mush and killed my respiratory system? Because my lungs and my brain didn't care that he was all kinds of levels of unattainable. They didn't care that there were about a thousand boss levels before I got anywhere near his league. And that was presuming I ever got out of best-friend's-weirdo-little-sister-zone.

Not that I wanted to.

Not really.

What the hell would I do if a guy like Kit ever looked at me twice?

I'd turn into a ridiculous puddle and that would be the end of it.

Besides, I wanted a guy who wanted a relationship. Right? Not just one night.

And guys like Kit did not want relationships. They only wanted one night.

So there it was. Easy to remember.

Kit was off-limits and out of my league. I was a hot mess and wanted something more.

"Say it with me now," I muttered to my lungs and my brain, hoping repetition would make it true.

6
Kit

I was starting to think maybe she didn't *hate me*, hate me. I wasn't going to suggest she liked me. But I was going to go out on a limb and suggest it wasn't that she hated me.

We saw it all the time with clients. Well, we saw it enough with clients.

Those ones who came to us for self-defence classes, the ones who looked over their shoulders all the time no matter where they were, the ones who felt something – someone – behind them no matter how safe they were, the ones who were running or hiding from something.

Amber was running or hiding from something. Or someone.

I couldn't remember a time when she wasn't the way she was, so I didn't think it was this last arsehole. But I couldn't think of anything that Hawk had mentioned that could be the cause of it.

But I knew what could help it.

It was amazing what a bit of confidence did for you.

I saw the transformation with all those people who came

to Tank for self-defence classes. They arrived with that uncertain demeanour, the one that masqueraded so well as indifference or aloofness. But once they were reminded they could protect themselves, they left looking happy, making eye contact, making plans, moving on.

A shrink would tell you that the lot of us at Grace Grayson Security could do with a couple of spoons of our own medicine. But our demons weren't exercised with a little self-defence. We had the ability to protect ourselves and others in almost any situation. We'd just been in enough situations to learn the hard way that you couldn't save everyone, no matter how good you were.

But if I was right, I could save Amber.

So I gave myself a new mission and it was going to start now.

I just wasn't sure exactly how to start.

But I did know where not to start. And it came with a stern reminder that Amber Grace was off-limits. Just because she'd actually looked at me for more than two milliseconds in a row, did not make it a lingering look and I had absolutely imagined the visceral tension between our locked gazes. Her lips parting did not mean she was thinking what I'd been thinking, B1. And her fingers on my skin had not been an invitation to reciprocate by throwing her against a wall and kissing the ever-living fuck out of her.

By the time Amber was walking back out of the other side of the house, I'd almost convinced myself of all of that. I was also fully dressed and Carmel was finishing off breakfast.

I'd told Carmel I could do it myself, but the damn woman had insisted for Amber's sake – she knew how well (or rather, poorly) I cooked.

She chattered at me in Spanish, berating me for not looking after Amber properly, for not looking after myself properly, for any number of things. And I let her, interjecting only with an apology or a defence.

I'd met Carmel on a mission years ago. We'd been stuck in Bolivia for months, hunted and harried. Carmel and her family had taken the team in. In payment, the people after us had killed her family and burnt down her house. But we'd got Carmel and her niece Flo out. Our commander at the time had sponsored them and I'd given them jobs when Hawk and I started the security company. Flo worked reception for us most days, although she was out on maternity leave at the moment – her partner had just had twin boys – and we were feeling her absence more than we liked to admit.

"Sorry, I left all my crap out again last night," Amber said slowly.

I looked over at the table and shook my head. "No, it's fine—"

"He never uses it anyway," Carmel interrupted. "I come in the morning and they've left cups and plates all over the coffee table. Pizza boxes everywhere. If Christopher had a dog, he would be very fat."

"I am trying to make a good impression here," I said to

her in Spanish and she laughed.

"There is something about this girl, no?" she replied in kind.

"No," I said firmly. "She's just my friend's sister. I'm doing her a favour."

"Oh, yes a favour," she chuckled knowingly.

"Yes, just a favour," I replied just as I heard Amber cry, "A-ha!" from behind us.

I turned and saw she was shaking her phone. Finally she shrugged and shoved it in her pocket.

"Ah, no admirers, *mija*," Carmel said to her.

Amber snorted and I watched her wrinkle her nose. "No. Thank God. But it is dead. Again. Although, the only person I *might* want to talk to is Pat and he seems averse to the things."

"Pat is Hawk, yes?" Carmel asked as she dished up breakfast.

"Yes," I answered.

"There's a definite resemblance between you two. With the hair–"

"She's got her great-grandfather's eyes," I said, knowing what always came next.

Amber and Hawk both had the sandy blond hair of their mum. But where Hawk's eyes were a shade between both parents' brown, Amber's were a blue that was almost violet. The family story was that their dad's grandfather had had violet eyes that charmed all the ladies. Hawk's suspicion was that his mum had an affair. But that was only after a few drinks and a few too many deaths. We'd never spoken about it again, but I'd never forgotten it.

Amber tucked her hair behind her ear subconsciously and, for the first time since I'd met Carmel, I wanted her gone. I wanted to know if my theory about Amber was right – the self-conscious thing, not the me imagining things thing. Although I had no idea how I was going to test it.

I didn't know what it was about Amber that morning, but I saw something in her I'd never seen before. Maybe it was because she'd never actually looked at me before. Maybe it was because we'd said more words that morning than I think we ever had in our whole lives. Maybe it was because I still felt her fingers on my bare skin like a persistent tingle. Maybe it was because I wanted her to not actually hate me so much that I was willing to imagine any other possibility. No matter how horrible.

"All right," Carmel sighed. "Anything I can do for you before I go, then?"

I blinked and realised there were two plates and two mugs of coffee in front of me. I smiled and shook my head. "No, that's plenty. Go and visit your nephews."

Carmel chuckled and waved me forward. I leant over the counter and let her kiss my cheeks the way she often did. "Lovely to meet you, Miss Amber. Leave your washing and a shopping list for me. I'll see you tomorrow if you're here."

Amber scoffed. "Ah, I'll no doubt be making more mess on Kit's dining table."

"That *is* a lot of paper."

Amber pushed her glasses up her nose and folded her arms around herself. "It's for my thesis."

"Oh, you're studying?"

Amber nodded. "PhD. Arthurian legend and classical romance." She gave that nod again.

Carmel looked at me. "A smart girl here."

I nodded at her. "Yes. Crazy smart. Always has been. Never fell for any of our jokes."

"Your 'jokes' were so obvious," Amber laughed. "No one was falling for them."

I looked to her and her smile shrunk. But it was still there, just more hesitant. The look in her eyes was soft and questioning. Again I felt her fingers on my skin and relived that moment of tension that had nothing to do with me worrying she hated me. In fact, it was the exact opposite. But I pushed it away.

"Let me walk you out," she said to Carmel, and I got cutlery out of the drawer while they went to the front door chatting.

I pulled myself onto one of the bar stools and set up the plates.

I heard an in-drawn breath and looked up to see Amber, half-frowning and paused like she'd been about to say something.

"What?" I asked her, indicating she sit down.

She practically had to climb up onto the barstool next to me. Once she was settled, she snuck a look at me. "No. Nothing. I just would have assumed you'd need to be at work by now."

I should have been. But it was a slow morning so I was going to take the time to try and peel away one of her infinite layers – if Nico could do it, it couldn't be that hard. Could it? Perhaps I'd just realise she really did just hate me. I was definitely, in no way thinking anything inappropriate about her.

I shrugged. "It's not that late."

She nodded as she started eating. "I guess."

"How's the study going?" I asked.

She looked at me out of the corner of her eye. "Fine."

I smirked, hoping to elicit another of those smiles. "Fine?"

"Fine." She nodded and seemed to fight a smile. A smile I was suddenly desperate to see again.

I looked at my plate in the hopes she wouldn't notice. "Hawk told us about Champers Day. Tank wanted us all to celebrate with you on Sunday."

She didn't say anything so I looked up and found her smirking. She was looking me right in the eye and I felt an excitement I didn't usually feel. I told myself it was only accomplishment. But there was this challenge and question and humour in her eyes I found it hard to ignore.

"What?" I asked, my own smile threatening to break through.

"Why do you lot not have normal names? Chaos, Hawk, Tank?"

"Rollie and Nico," I finished and she laughed.

"I actually feel sorry for Nico. Unless he was born Reginald or something?"

I looked down at my plate as I smiled. "No. He was born Nicholas."

"He seemed really nice. Who did he friendly fire to not get a nickname?"

I was enjoying this side of her. I didn't know what had brought it out. But I'd never seen it directed at me before and I was enjoying it. Knowing I was the one who was making her smile – okay, maybe at Nico's expense – was a singular feeling after all those years of indifference. Do you know how hard it is on a guy when he feels like he has to choose between his best mate and his little sister? I could see the strain it had taken on Hawk over the years and, if I could remedy it, then I would. All that other stuff that was all in my head would get over itself.

"Ah, well. Nico does have a nickname."

Her eyes widened and she looked at me expectantly. "What is it? I have never heard Pat use it."

I grinned. "We only use it over comms." Or when we were making salacious jokes at his expense, obviously.

"Why? Is it scandalous?" she gasped, her eyes shining brighter than I'd ever seen them.

I shook my head as I sat back with my coffee. "We used to call him Overlord. He's always been the tech guy, usually at base, barking instructions at us over the comms and the name kinda stuck. But over time, that unfortunately shortened to O Lord–"

She snorted. And, evidenced by the fact her hand flew to her face, I think she lost a little coffee along with that. She stared at me, eyes wide and inquisitive, her hand still over the lower part of her face. I nodded, enjoying this moment between us.

"Oh, yes. The jokes became endless. Between Rollie moaning at him over comms and your brother counting off how many orgasms he had with each bullseye… Well we save that stuff for jobs, now. Give Nico some respite."

"Because I'm sure you're far too sensible for orgasm jokes," she said teasingly.

I kicked my head to the side. "Of course. Orgasms aren't a joking matter. I thought, as a woman, you'd take these things more seriously," I teased.

Weirdly, she shrugged and pushed her glasses up her nose before picking up her coffee mug. "I don't know that I qualify for a vote to be honest," she said before taking a sip.

I blinked and watched her for a few seconds. "What? Why?"

"I would assume only the O Lords minions got a vote in whether orgasms are to be joked about or not."

I was still confused. Was she referring to Nico now or…? "Are you saying you've never had an orgasm?" I blurted out like a complete numpty.

Her cheeks coloured and it was something like the third time ever I'd seen them do that. She cleared her throat and put down her mug. "Uh. Yeah."

"You've been with the wrong guys, Amber," I scoffed.

She tucked a piece of hair behind her ear and snuck a look at me. "I technically haven't been with any guys, Christopher."

My mouth dropped open and I stared at her.

She was twenty-three and she wasn't unattractive. How was she still a virgin? I mean, the geek thing was a little lost on me. Always had been. Until this week when I still didn't get the geek think but I got the Amber thing. But to never have…? And to not even have…? Even by herself…?

"What?" I spluttered.

She shrugged nonchalantly, but there was some of that self-consciousness in her. "I thought it was common knowledge."

"Common knowledge?" I laughed, but there was no real humour in it. "You think Hawk talks to us about that stuff?"

She shrugged and wouldn't look at me again. I reached out to her and put my finger under her chin. She let me turn her head to face me and I tried to catch her eyes.

"Amber, I swear he's never mentioned it."

Her eyes flew up to mine and the breath was knocked out of me for a moment. I couldn't remember a time we'd ever looked at each other in the eye, and now we'd gone and done it twice in one morning. I'd seen her eyes plenty, but she'd always been avidly not looking at mine. Now though. Now she wasn't just looking at me, she was staring into my eyes and I saw something in there I'd wanted to see. But now I'd seen it, I wished I hadn't. Even if it did take my mind off thinking about her fingers on my ribs.

Something was hurting her and it tugged on something in me. I didn't know how I was going to help her. I just knew I had to try.

"Amber…?" I said softly.

Her eyes widened for a moment and she pulled away, clearing her throat and pushing up her glasses; an action I was starting to see as defensive. "Yeah?" she asked as she went back to her breakfast.

I didn't know how or where to start. "How are you doing?"

She threw me a look. "You a shrink now?"

I huffed. "No. And I know we've never really…"

"Spoken. Acknowledged each other. Got along?" she offered and I had serious déjà vu. But she'd lost some tension and the rueful humour was back in her eyes.

"Fuck, you're your brother's sister," I muttered.

"What?"

I shook my head. "Nothing. All that. But I'm here if you need anything."

She looked me over and I wondered what she saw now.

When Hawk and I had been teenagers, we hadn't given her the best example. We'd gone out late, we'd hooked up with girls all over the place, we drank, we smoked, we were your typical early 2000s juvenile try-hard delinquents. As we got older, not a lot had changed I guessed. Our sleeping habits hadn't got any better, we slept with as many women as we could get our hands on, we drank, we didn't really smoke anymore. The only thing that had really changed was that we were now deadly with multiple weapons and forms of combat. Oh, and we had money to waste on our varied and numerous vices.

I couldn't really have said what image that gave her of me. And what my offer did to that image. Did she think I was just pandering, being facetious? Did she know I was being honest, that I would do anything for me and mine? Sure, she wasn't technically mine. Because I wasn't allowed to even consider thinking that way. But she was of mine so same difference really. Happy sister, happy brother.

Slowly, she nodded. "Thanks, Kit. I'm… Going to be okay. I have my thesis to work on. I have a Carmel now. I'm good."

I searched her eyes before she looked away. "Okay. Well, offer stands."

She nodded. "Sure. Thanks."

I didn't want to leave. I wanted to stay and work out what was going on in her head. I wanted to stop my best mate's little sister hurting. But I had a job. A job which let me invite her to stay and be taken care of. So I kind of needed to make sure I didn't lose it. Not that I'd be fired. But our clients could piss off if we pissed them off.

"Your brother will no doubt beat the crap out of me if I'm much later," I said, pushing myself up. "I'll see you later."

Amber looked up at me and nodded. "Sure. No worries."

"Have a good day."

"You too, Kit." She gave me a smile and I nodded before

I headed out.

My day and the next were the same as usual. I had self-entitled clients wanting things we weren't obliged to give them, there were bank issues because always, there were legitimate threats to clients we had to deal with. I'd had to have a couple of fights with some guys and I'd got more blood on my shirt that Carmel was going to kill me over if I didn't remember to soak it.

Still I got home in the wee hours of Friday morning. I walked in to most of the lights off, so I'd guessed Amber was already in bed. As I walked past the table, I stopped to see what pattern she'd put her notes in that day. I had no idea if it was a way to measure her progress, but I knew she'd been busy based on the fact that everything would be spread out in a different way.

I was just about to move into my bedroom when I heard her screaming. Panic lanced through me and I was halfway to her room before I noticed what I was doing.

7

Amber

I felt hands on my shoulders.

"No!" I yelled and sat up. I had to get away. "No!" I had to get away.

"Amber?" a voice I recognised cut through the frantic beating of my heart and the wild noise in my head.

I realised I was still in bed. As I took in my surroundings, I registered Kit was sitting beside me, his face full of worry. He was still dressed so he mustn't have been home long. I blinked and looked into those rich brown eyes.

"Amber? Are you okay?" he asked me.

I nodded, but I noticed I was still shaking. That desperate need to have a shower, to be clean, clawed at me as the fragments of memory combined with the leftovers of my dream and made me feel sick. I was cold and hot all at the same time.

"Are you sure?"

I nodded again but felt like I was going to throw up. I ran to the bathroom and just got to the toilet as I gagged. But nothing came out. I panted heavily, not sure if I was still going to be sick or not.

"What's wrong? What can I do?" Kit asked, dropping beside me.

I shook my head at him. "It'll pass."

"This has happened before." It wasn't a question.

I nodded, not trusting myself to speak yet.

It had happened before. It had been a regular occurrence for years. But after years of therapy and medication, it had finally gone away and I'd thought I'd seen the end of it. Apparently all the avoiding of my issues the last few days had dredged it all back up again.

"What do you need?" Kit asked.

I needed a shower. I needed water. I needed more sleep than I'd been letting myself have. I needed Kit to stop being…whatever he'd been this last week.

Kit had never been kind or sweet or funny. He'd been brooding and sexy and angry. But this week he was nothing like that. He exuded everything that screamed bad boy under those suits, but like he had a squishy soft centre in the middle. And that I couldn't handle. I was barely reminding my lungs and brain not to go to mush around him, I didn't need my heart threatening to do the same.

"Amber, what can I do?"

I couldn't answer. My heart was threatening to pound out of my chest and I felt like I was about to stop breathing. And neither of those things currently had anything to do with Kit. I pushed myself up on shaky legs and took a step towards the shower. But my stupid legs buckled. Kit, of course, was there to catch me with those stupidly strong arms.

"Tell me how to help," he pleaded.

"Shower," I wheezed, my skin crawling. It would take everything I had not to scrub my skin raw from head to toe.

He nodded, reached over to drop the toilet seat and lid, and directed me to sit on it. "We're going to do this together, okay?" he said in calm, comforting tones. "I'm just going to take off my jacket," he said slowly as he did so and we both ignored him taking off his holster, "my tie, my belt, my shoes… And my socks…" He crouched in front of me and kept speaking calmly and comfortingly. "You okay?" I nodded. "Good. Now, I'm going to turn on the water. Just shake or nod in answer. Do you want it cold?" I shook. "Tepid?" Another shake. "Warm?" Another shake. "Hot?" I nodded. "Good. Sit tight and I'll be back in just a second, okay?"

I nodded again and tried hard to focus on reminding myself that each breath was not my last. He got up slowly and went to turn the water on. Then he was back and helping me stand up.

"You okay to walk?" he asked and I nodded.

He helped me into the shower and got in with me, still in his suit pants and shirt. My legs buckled again and he caught me again.

"Shall we sit?" he asked softly and I nodded yet again. "Okay. I'll sit, then your turn."

One more nod.

He dropped down and held his hands out to me. I was on autopilot. I took his hands and let him settle me in his lap, his arms tightly around me like he could protect me from the world. I curled up against him, feeling an inordinate amount of comfort from the steady beating of his heart against my cheek.

"Your brother was a right tosser today, you know," he said in that calm, comforting voice as he leant his cheek on my head. "He hid Nico's tablet, which freaked the poor nerd out well and truly. Then he lumped his client on me which meant I had to send Tank to mine when he should have been taking a class…"

And Kit just prattled on about his day. Always in that calm, steady voice, the hot water falling around us. In the midst of an already fairly epic freak out, I had no time to freak out about the fact that I was in Kit's arms in the shower. I also had no time to freak out about the fact I was in Kit's arms in the shower having a freak out.

And slowly, as he just talked about seemingly nothing and held me, my heart calmed down, the nausea abated and my breathing evened out. My skin even lost that crawling feeling; I'd taken layers upon layers of skin off in the past because of that crawling feeling and it made me mad to ignore it, but I knew it would be better in the end.

Kit obviously realised when my breathing was back to normal as he rubbed my back and dropped his face towards mine. "Better?"

I nodded against him. "I'm sorry."

"For what?"

"For…that. It hasn't been that bad for a…long time."

He tipped my chin up to look at me. "How often does it happen?"

"It used to be pretty regular. But it stopped a couple of years ago."

He frowned and I hated the pain I saw in his eyes. I hated even more it was because of me. "Hawk never mentioned it."

I looked down again. "He doesn't know."

"How?"

"I'm fine, Kit."

"Amber, I know a sign of PTSD when I see it…"

I didn't doubt he did.

I rested my head on his chest again. "We didn't want him to worry. You guys were so busy. Risking your lives. He didn't need to be thinking of me at home."

Kit scoffed and held me tighter. "He always thought of you at home. We all did. Fucker would have died fifty times over if we weren't thinking of you."

I pushed away from him enough to look at him properly. "What?"

He smiled, but there was still sadness in his eyes. "All Hawk cared about was coming home to you. And we all cared about Hawk, so we all cared about him coming home to you. I lost count of the times I did the polytrauma stint and the rehab instead of him."

Horror flooded me. "No. No. If I'd known."

He took my face in his hands and smiled at me. And this time, it reached his eyes and it felt like my heart re-started. "None of us would ever have had it any other way. We were brothers and we looked after our own." He brushed my hair back and dropped his hands to wrapping around me again.

"*Gratia dei per chao…*" I whispered, reverently. By the grace of chaos.

"Exactly. I was nothing without him anyway."

"That's not true," I said before I could caution myself.

"What?"

I'd started now. "That's not true. You're plenty without him."

"Like what?"

Damn. I couldn't very well tell him that he'd been the world to me for years. That he was in danger of becoming the world to me again if I didn't remember who he was, who I was. It didn't matter if there was another side to him or not. He was off-limits.

"I don't know," I said softly.

There was a shift in the mood.

"Do you want to talk about?" he asked.

"About what?"

"Whatever happened that gives you these episodes."

I huffed a laugh. "My boyfriend and my best friend went behind my back."

His hand ran up and down my back gently. "Before that." It was a reprimand but I could also tell he wouldn't push me if I didn't want to be pushed.

"Did you work with hostages or something?" I blurted out.

"Sort of. We dealt with a lot of people. And most of them were terrified and hurt and in so much pain there was nothing we could do. But we never gave up."

We found each other's eyes again and I wasn't sure exactly what I saw in his, but I could see something had changed him. There was pain deep inside now where before there'd only been…emptiness and a different sort of pain. Before they'd left, Kit had been trying to find his place in the world. Now he looked like he'd found it, but the truth was much too real.

"I was attacked," I told him.

I felt his hands tighten on me. "What?"

I nodded. "Uh. It was a little after you guys finished your special ops training I think. Pat said you were off to Beirut maybe?" I huffed a small, humourless laugh because it was better than crying. "Dannie, Farrah and I went to a party at Travis' house. And uh… There was this guy there. We… We danced and drank. I don't remember how we got to the bedroom…but, when I realised what he wanted, I tried to fight back. I got a fair few bruises for my efforts and I still have a couple of scars. But I kneed him before…" My breath hitched and I couldn't go on.

But I was pretty sure Kit didn't need me to.

He pulled me closer to him and it was the most accepted I'd ever felt.

On the rare occasion I'd told anyone that story, they'd

looked at me like I was broken or dirty and they'd avoided touching me. It had been obvious in the way they withdrew. Dannie had witnessed the last bit of it all, so she'd known everything. But even she'd had trouble dealing with it.

Apparently though, not Kit. Kit, who stories said went through every girl in his year, half the ones above and below and all the teachers under thirty-five by the time he left school. I never knew how many of the stories were true, but some of them had to be if he'd got the reputation in the first place.

But that guy, on hearing my story, only held me close, kissed my hair and said, "I'm so sorry, Amber."

I sniffled. "It wasn't your fault."

"No. It wasn't. But I'm sorry Hawk and I weren't here to help you, to beat that sorry excuse for a human being to a fucking pulp." He paused. "Is that why…?"

I knew was he was asking and I didn't mind that he was asking. "I don't know. Sometimes I think yes. Sometimes I think the right guy hasn't come along. Sometimes I think maybe I'm just broken in all sorts of ways."

He squeezed me tightly. "You're not broken, Amber. Not…" He sighed. "Not when you're still looking, when you haven't given up."

I felt like I knew what he wasn't saying there.

"Not like you?" I asked.

I felt his breath catch. "Not like me," he finally agreed.

"You saw some terrible stuff?" I asked.

I felt him nod. "Saw it. Did it. Had it done to us."

"Would you change any of it?"

He shook his head. "No. We did some really amazing things, met some really amazing people. But it's the price you pay. You can't get something for nothing."

I nodded. "I guess not." Then something caught my eye and I pulled away.

"What?" he asked.

"Are you bleeding?"

He looked down at the pink smudge on his shirt. "Ah. No. That's not mine." He frowned for a moment. "I don't think."

Without thinking, I started undoing his buttons.

"Woah, what are you doing?"

"I'm going to rinse this out so Carmel doesn't yell at you again."

He grinned at me ruefully as he helped me get him out of the shirt. It stuck to his skin something shocking with all the water. But we finally got it off him and I shifted slightly to hold it under the stream of hot water.

"Cold water!" Kit laughed and I looked at him quizzically. His smile softened as he took the shirt from me. "Cold water or the blood will congeal."

"That's something I didn't realise I didn't need to know," I replied, not even bothering to fight my return smile.

Our eyes locked again and my heart fluttered. My mouth went dry. My teeth caught my lip like they knew I was going to say or do something stupid. It wasn't just that Kit was gorgeous. It wasn't just that the humour in his eyes was infectious. It wasn't just that being near him did funny things to my entire being. He'd understood me in a way no one else had. It was this insistent feeling I had that something was zinging between us. It was this niggling sensation that something had changed between us. But what? And was it all just me?

"Carmen'll yell at me if she finds out you rinsed it for me anyway," he said softly as his eyes searched mine lingeringly, and I entertained the notion he felt the same way I did.

I sniffed away a laugh. "Well, are you going to tell her?"

He shrugged. "No, but she just knows these things."

I smiled. "You know you would have thrown it in the hamper and forgotten about it."

It seemed one of Carmel's favourite talking points; how often she had to get blood out of Kit's shirts. I'd had a lengthy conversation with her about earlier in the day when she'd come by.

"Yeah, probably."

I suddenly started to feel self-conscious and I looked down. Which only made me more self-conscious as I realised my nipples were standing loud and proud through my t-shirt. And I knew it wasn't just the chill of the air to blame. I felt my cheeks heat and took a deep breath.

"Right. Uh… I think I'm good."

Kit nodded. "All right. Count of three."

I took his shirt back from him in confusion. "What? Oh!"

I yelped as his hands were on my hips and he somehow managed to get me to standing.

I squished myself against the wall as he jumped up. He took my face in his hands again and looked at me seriously. My stomach clenched and my heart skipped. And it was only doubled when he spoke, his voice fierce and passionate.

"You're not broken. You're all the more amazing because you kept going. If you need anything – *anything* – I'm here for you, okay?"

I could only nod as he searched my eyes and I hoped he couldn't tell my heart was fluttering madly. Finally, he seemed happy with my answer.

He kissed my forehead much like Patrick was wont to do, then reached behind me and turned the taps off.

"You want to go first or shall I?"

I looked up at him in panic.

"Well, we're going to want to get out of these wet clothes. There are plenty of towels, but I assume you want to go one at a time. I've been told I have a cute arse, but you might feel self-conscious about me seeing yours."

I smiled and swatted him with his shirt. "You can go first then. I'll close my eyes."

His grin was totally swoon-worthy. "I'll forgive you if you peek." His eyes trailed down my body quickly, he winked, then got out of the shower.

I am slightly ashamed to admit I did peek a little and he did in fact have just as nice an arse in nothing as he did in his suit pants. He put his shirt in the sink and turned on the tap. Then he waited in my room with the door closed while I struggled off my wet clothes, dropped them with his in the bath, dried off and wrapped a towel around me. I turned the sink tap off and opened the bathroom door.

"I don't need babysitting," I said to him when I saw him sitting on my bed, looking at his phone. Although, I didn't hate that he was still there.

"No. You don't. I just didn't want you to feel abandoned."

My heart warmed unnervingly. "Oh…"

"You right to get to sleep?"

"Have you eaten?"

He grinned at me. "You know I haven't."

"I'll get dressed and join you?"

He nodded and stood up. "Yeah, I'd like that."

Just before he left, I said, "Kit?"

He turned and I forced my eyes off the way the towel hung low on his hips. "Yeah?"

"Maybe… Maybe Tank could teach me self-defence?"

He looked me over carefully and I wondered what was going through his head. "Will you let me?" he finally asked.

My chest fluttered. I'd read enough trashy romances where those sorts of training moments turn sexual. But I hadn't met Tank despite all the stories I'd heard of him – he was the huge monster out of them, rampaging through everything and scaring even the hardened terrorists – and I trusted Kit.

So I nodded. "Of course."

A smile lit his face. "Great. I've got most of Saturday off, shall we start then?"

I nodded again. "Sure."

"Okay. I'll see you out there in a bit. Want a whiskey?"

I smiled softly. "Yeah, thanks."

He gave one nod and headed out while I got changed.

8

Kit

I'd woken up to hear noises in the kitchen.

I rolled over and saw it was barely seven on my alarm clock – not that I ever used it as an alarm. I frowned and pulled myself out of bed. I stumbled out of my room to see Amber in the kitchen in nothing but one of my huge bath sheets, her wet hair tumbling around her shoulders and a flash of red at her shoulders. I stood outside the kitchen and just watched her. I don't think I'd ever seen her with her hair down. Not in…at least ten years.

She was cooking and…was she dancing?

Yes, as she was moving around the kitchen she looked like she was singing to herself and she was swaying her hips. She was the most relaxed I'd seen her…ever.

"Morning," I rasped.

And that wasn't just desire's effect on me. My brain might have worked as soon as I was awake, my voicebox less so.

She jumped and turned, her hand flying to her chest. She looked me over and her lips parted. For a moment, I was

103

convinced she was thinking what I was thinking. There was a flash of something very like desire on her face and something deep in me felt it. Then she huffed self-deprecatingly and I felt like I must have still been dreaming.

"Hi. I…uh…" She looked around and waved the spatula in her other hand. "I thought I'd… For last night…" She coloured and looked down.

I smiled. "You didn't have to."

"No, I know." She threw me a smile. "But I wanted to."

I pulled myself onto one of the barstools and ran my hand through my hair.

We'd talked for a while the previous night over a couple of glasses of whiskey. Dinner had been a comfortable silence, but then we'd slowly started chatting. As in, we actually chatted and she'd legitimately laughed out loud a couple of times and she'd teased me the same way she teased Hawk. It meant we were both running on very little sleep, but I could live with that.

For the first time in years, we'd got along. I was going to say, with almost complete confidence, that she didn't hate me anymore. I still wasn't confident she liked me. But she didn't hate me.

I hated that *that* was the moment we'd shared that got us to that point. I hated that she was hurting. I hated what had happened to her. But I was happy that I'd been able to help her, I was happy that she'd let me, I was happy that she'd asked for more, and I was happy that it had got us to the point where she looked almost completely natural in my kitchen.

"Oh, yeah. Sorry about… I was up later, then showered longer… And I wasn't sure what time you'd be up. So I wanted to…before you were up," she rambled and I couldn't help but smile.

"It's fine. You live here, too. Be comfortable."

She shot me a quick, sincere smile before she got some milk out of the fridge. As she closed it and stepped away, the towel fell off. Well it obviously got caught in the fridge door and, as she stepped away, it was pulled off her. The semantics, at the time were lost on me, though.

And I think the sight I got was actually worse than if she'd been completely naked under there. She was wearing this skimpy little bright red lingerie and it fit her to perfection in every way.

Last time I'd seen that much of her skin…she would have been… Fuck. Maybe fourteen? She'd barely had boobs and certainly hadn't had hips. Nearly ten years later, she had both in abundance and I couldn't drag my eyes off her.

Her hips were wide, curving up to a gorgeous waist. Her breasts were large, firm and perky. It had been a while since I'd had to worry about inconvenient boners. But this wasn't just inconvenient. She might not have hated me, but she certainly didn't like me and there was the small matter of her being my best friend's little sister, so there was nothing appropriate about it even if it was just a purely biological reaction. I might have envisioned a few moments in the last few days, but that was hardly justification.

She'd closed her eyes and held up a hand to stop me saying anything. But I don't think I would have been able to anyway.

"I know. I know," she sighed. "But it's all I had left. Okay. No. It was the least scandalous of what I had left."

Because that was going to help the raging hard on in my pants.

I was over trying to tell myself it was inappropriate. Amber wasn't just an attractive young woman, she was also sweet and witty and had a razor sharp mind, and she'd survived something horrible with all of that intact. So I wasn't going to torment myself for being attracted to her. But I was a grown arsed man and I could keep them to myself – I hoped.

She bent down and grabbed the towel, wrapping it back around herself.

"I just wasn't thinking when I stormed out of there. I, for some reason, cleaned out my lingerie drawer, grabbed a few pairs of pants and some jumpers." She rolled her eyes at herself.

"The rest of your stuff is there still," I said and I hadn't heard my voice that strangled since I was about seventeen. I wasn't even sure if it was a statement or a question.

How the hell did I not know that Amber was hiding that under all those oversized jumpers? How the hell had I not noticed last night? And more interestingly, *I'd still been thinking inappropriately about her before I knew it was there…*

She looked at me from the corner of her eye as she went back to breakfast. "Yeah. The rest of my clothes, my books, my console, my…everything…" she huffed, then was sliding two plates full of bacon and eggs towards me before she finished coffee.

"Are you going back to get it?" I asked, wishing I had more control over my voice.

I'd been told I had this sexy quality to it first thing in the morning. There was nothing sexy about sounding like a horny teenager though. Thankfully, she didn't seem to notice.

She breathed heavily and put her hands on the bench for a second. "If I could bring myself to face that raging bitch, yes."

"What about tomorrow?"

She looked at me over her shoulder and I told myself I wasn't picturing her without the towel on. I swallowed hard.

"What about tomorrow?" she asked. "I thought you were going to start teaching me self-defence?"

"I plan to do that." And keep my hands to myself. "But we've all got tomorrow morning off. Would five hulking wankers help your case? We could do the self-defence thing on Sunday instead?"

She broke into a wide sincere smile as she leant over the bench towards me. "You offering up your security team to help me pack up my stuff?" she teased.

I felt myself falling into gear. I was less horny teenager

and more practiced man again. "Well our job is protection. We also happen to be very good at manual labour."

She looked me over with a wry smirk. "All right. And how much would that cost me?"

"Well, the roommate of the CEO surely gets perks?" I asked coyly.

Her eyes fucking shone with humour and I felt elated. "Perks?" she sniggered. "God, what does the CEO's woman get?"

I laughed. "Roommate is the top of the hierarchy. His woman's going to have to deal with it."

She smiled. "Well, I'll bet she'll love that."

"If any woman was unlucky enough to end up with me, she's going to have to accept you're here to stay."

"Unlucky?" she asked, passing me a coffee as she got onto the stool beside me.

I nodded. "Unlucky."

"Pfft. You're a catch Christopher Barrett Grayson. And anyone who tells you otherwise deserves to lose their perks." She pointed at me and I was happier than I needed to be that she was this assertive self with me now.

This is how she'd always been with Hawk and I'd caught glimpses of it over the years, seen her unable to hide it sometimes even. It was one of the things that had made sure I never questioned Hawk's love for her, never questioned why we had to keep him safe, what made me invite her to stay. And here she was saying I was a catch.

"A catch? How am I a catch?" I snorted.

She coloured again and looked at me through her eyelashes. "You just are."

"I just am?" I asked and she nodded. Completely without thinking about it, I reached over a tickled her and she laughed. "I just am? That's a terrible explanation."

She looked up at me and my fingers stopped, but I didn't take my hands off her.

My heart thudded. My breath felt a little less easy.

The moment sizzled with unspoken…everything. It was one of those moments you kiss the girl, dammit. Only I didn't kiss the girl. I had to firmly remind myself I was imagining that the girl wanted to be kissed. But it wasn't easy. The way she looked into my eyes, the look in hers, the soft smile at her lips. I didn't even have words for it. It was all feeling. And it felt amazing. Forbidden, but amazing. This was definitely a kissing moment, but the knowledge I shouldn't was stronger. Just.

"You're not the guy who left, Kit. That guy was…" She looked down and pushed her glasses up her nose. She cleared her throat. "That guy was almost a catch. The guy who came back? Well, he's even more."

My chest warmed and I wasn't sure it was in a way it was supposed to, or even a way it ever had before. But I liked it and I wasn't putting a stop to it.

Had she never hated me? Had we just been awkward around each other because we didn't understand each other? I still didn't understand all that study or anything, but it wasn't difficult with her like it used to be.

She looked up at me, her eyes boring into mine, and I had that moment again. I had that moment where I could almost see a different life for myself, where I could imagine what it would have been like if we'd always got along. That protectiveness rose up in me and I cupped her cheek.

Her eyes widened a little and she took a breath, but I smiled at her. She lay her hand over mine and I really felt like it was one of those kiss the girl moments. But that wasn't what I wanted this moment to be. It was more than that.

"You're better to me than I deserve," I told her softly.

"No. I just know you better than I should." But she smiled too before she turned away slowly, and we ate breakfast while we chatted.

It was nice. In fact, it was really nice. It was even nice enough that I stopped torturing myself with that imagined first kiss over and over again. For most minutes in the hour.

****

I looked at the centre screen in my car as though I could see them. "We serious right now?"

"Yeah. Let's call McLean and see if we can get a table. Take her out properly," Tank said.

"You've never done Champers Day. How would you know what's proper?" Rollie asked.

I pictured Tank shrugging. "Why can't we make our own Champers Day?"

"I think she'd like it," Nico said and I pictured him behind his screen as usual.

I wondered exactly what they'd talk about. He'd all but said they'd got on. Now I wondered exactly how *well* they'd got on.

"Why don't we all suit up, take her out, and make her feel super special?" Hawk said.

"Small problem. What's she going to wear?" I asked as I pulled up at the lights.

"Exactly what are you saying about my little sister, man?" Hawk laughed.

"I'm just wondering how many evening gowns she's got at the back of her closet."

"I'll call Petra, get her to open. You take her tonight and pick something for Sunday?"

"Who's calling McLean?" I asked.

"I'm on it," Tank said.

I nodded as the traffic kept moving. "Okay. Ask him if he's got that table—"

"He's gone," Rollie sniggered. "McLean's already looking for a table, I'll bet."

I nodded as I turned into the Mayhew's parking garage. "Yeah. All right. Let me know if we've got the table. If he needs reminding about that time we—"

"It's fine. We've got his best table all Sunday night," Tank called, sounding like he was on the other side of the room.

"Okay. And...?"

"Petra's open until you need her," Hawk called.

"Okay. We're doing this. Black tie, boys?" I asked.

"Yep," they all chorused.

"Okay. You'll all be at the penthouse in the morning?"

"Operation Save Bert's Shit is a go from 0800," Hawk replied.

"All right. Take the night off, you wankers. I'll see you in the morning."

"Sounds good, boss-man," Rollie said and they hung up on me.

I turned off the car and headed up the lift. Thankfully, Mrs Fortescue had had a falling out with Mrs Barry and decided not to go to whatever gala I'd been supposed to take her to.

"Night, Mr Grayson."

I nodded. "Night, Nigel." As I stepped into the penthouse, I looked around. "Amber?"

"Yeah?" she called from the direction of her room.

"You dressed?"

"Uh, odd question. But yes."

I headed down to her room and leant in her doorway to find her looking for something in her drawer.

"Come on, we're heading out."

She looked up at me in surprise. "What? Why?"

I nodded. "I just need to change, then we need to get a move on."

She blinked. "What should I...? Wait, aren't you working?"

I shook my head and started moving to my room. "My job was cancelled. We're going out, but we need to make a stop first."

"Uh, okay… Do I need to change?" she asked, following me.

I shook my head as I loosened my tie. "No. It'll be fine. Give me two minutes."

I threw a look back to her and saw her nodding. "Uh. Okay."

It didn't take me long to swap my suit for some jeans and a hoody to match hers.

"Are you sure I'm—"

I nodded as I pushed up my sleeves. "Perfect. Come on."

I strode out and she hurried along behind me. When the lift came back, Nigel was obviously surprised.

"Mr Grayson." He nodded.

"Nigel. This is Miss Grace."

Nigel smiled to Amber. "Miss Grace.

"Hi," she said to him, then her hand was on my arm. "Do I need to know where we're going?"

I shook my head and gave her a small smile. "No. You're fine. I promise."

I watched her nod and she pulled away.

I took her elbow as we crossed the lobby.

"Oh, Miss Grace. Wonderful to see you!" the old guy at the door called.

"You too, Johnson," she replied as we wandered past.

"How do you know him? I didn't think you'd left?"

"I haven't. But he was the one who found me standing in the rain and said I could call Pat from the foyer."

I nodded and smiled at her. "So I have him to thank for my new roommate?"

She grinned. "Thank or blame?"

"You said his name was Johnson?" I asked and she nodded.

I was going to remember the guy who'd been responsible for all this.

"Amber!" I heard a voice call as we came down the Mayhew's front steps and I started directing her left.

I followed Amber's gaze and saw a young woman who may well have been Dannie all grown up. I put my hand on Amber's back in support as she stopped and the woman rushed over.

"I've been trying to get hold of you all week. Where have you been?" she said and I saw she was more interested in trying to catch my attention than she was seeking Amber's forgiveness.

Typical Dannie.

"I've been busy. I've been safe," Amber replied.

"She's staying with me," I told Dannie, my voice hard; cheating I could not abide, and betrayal was worse.

Dannie looked me over, then she gave me what I'm sure was supposed to be a winning smile. "Chaos Grayson?"

"Chaos?" another voice sniggered and I looked over to see some shrivelled dickweed.

I felt Amber tense and she stepped closer to me. I didn't

have to be a genius to guess who this guy was. He was small, he was weedy, and there was a glint in his eyes that told me he was used to getting what he wanted. Probably by throwing Daddy's money around.

"What kind of name is Chaos?" the guy scoffed.

My eyes narrowed and he lost a fair chunk of his bluster.

"Kit's letting me stay with him for a while…" Amber said and I hated that these people were making her feel small.

I could see the guy looking between us like he was trying to work out what we were to each other. I wrapped my arm around her shoulder protectively and, if I'm honest, a little possessively.

"We should go," I said to her. "We need to be at McLean's by eight." Sure, on Sunday, but they didn't need to know that.

"I–" Amber started and my arm tightened around her gently to shush her.

Dannie's mouth dropped open. "McLean's? You're taking her to McLean's?"

The dickweed scoffed derisively. "And who the hell are you?"

I let go of Amber and took a step towards him. He shrunk away.

"Someone you don't want to cross," I snarled.

"Leave it, babe," Dannie said to him, pawing at his arm, and I glared at her.

But she wasn't worth the waste of words. I took Amber's

hand and pulled her along. Petra's little boutique was only a few buildings away. So Dannie and the dickweed would probably see us going in. But that would give them something to think about. Let him think she was mine now. See how he liked that.

"Kit, where are we?" Amber asked and I heard the tremor in her voice. "Did you just say we were going to McLean's?"

I whirled to face her and cupped her cheek. "No one can make you feel inferior without your consent. Don't give them your consent. They don't deserve it."

She nodded and gave me a small smile. I could see the confusion in her eyes but out here was not the place to put them to rest.

"Come on," I said, taking her hand again and tugging her after me.

I let go of her and knocked on Petra's door. Petra's head popped into view and she beamed when she saw us. As she unlocked the door for us, I looked back and saw Dannie and the dickweed watching us. I didn't take my eyes off them until Amber was safely inside the shop.

"Oh, look at you!" Petra squealed in excitement as she took Amber's hands. She threw a look to me. "And what does this gorgeous creature need, Chaos?"

I smirked. "Black tie. Full evening gown. To go."

Petra sighed at Amber like they were in on some joke. "He does like to create challenges. Still they don't call him Chaos for nothing. Now, colours?"

Petra looked between us and I could see Amber was feeling overwhelmed and confused. But even then, she was gorgeous and there was a touch of humour to her confusion that she turned on me.

"Start with blue," I suggested.

Amber looked at me with barely concealed panic. "What?"

"A dress, love," Petra said kindly. "Chaos, did you just drag this poor beauty in here?"

I shrugged. Petra knew me too well. "The boys and I are taking Amber to McLean's on Sunday."

Amber frowned. "But you told–"

I shrugged. "Let them think what they will."

"Oh, McLean's," Petra giggled. "With five big strapping dates? Yes please." She grunted in a way that reminded me she wasn't just what this shop made her look. "God, Tank in a tux."

"Keep it in your pants, woman," I laughed. "It's Amber appreciation night. I promise I'll send him in here under some pretence sometime next week. Your choice of outfit."

She shot me a devilish grin and turned to Amber. "What size are you, love?" she asked as she led Amber over to the racks of dresses.

I dropped into one of the curtesy chairs they had around the place for just this purpose. Although, I'd never brought a woman in here who wasn't a client. And usually it was me getting fitted for something.

My tension melted away as I watched Petra's natural

charm win Amber over. Soon the two of them were laughing like they'd known each other for years. But Petra was just like that. Much like the Grace Grayson team, Petra was hardened on the inside and shiny on the outside. I would never have gone so far as to describe her as a shiny turd – Rollie yes, Petra no – but she was adept at only showing the necessary parts of her personality.

I checked my phone as I watched them, looking over emails, catching up on the news.

"You have to be shitting me!" Amber yelled and I looked up. She was staring at me accusingly. "You are not spending this much money on a dress for me!"

"I am. Pick something." I smiled as she opened and closed her mouth a couple of times. "Do you want me to get Hawk here to pick for you?" I could see just how tempting an idea she found that.

She turned to Petra. "So, uh… You said the navy one would look nice?" I heard her say.

They took a few off the rack and Petra took her to the fitting rooms to do her thing. I took care of a few business details while I waited, ignoring how weird it felt to be at the boutique in my casual gear.

After a while, I heard Petra saying, "See, it drapes so nicely on you here."

I looked up and was out of my seat before I'd managed to scoop my chin off the floor.

Amber's hair hung in waves down her back. I hadn't realised that morning how long it was. But the dress. It was a dark navy blue. The back was just three strands of ribbon keeping the front to her body. The skirt hung in swathes of fabric, hugging her hips and tumbling elegantly to the ground. As she turned, I saw there was a split in the fabric up to her mid-thigh and Petra had paired it with some nude heels.

She looked amazing and my breath was completely knocked out of me. Don't get me wrong, there was nothing wrong with the oversized jumpers and the jeans. Amber had a way of pulling those off with that sweet geeky-chic that gave new meaning to the term sexy librarian. But there was something about the look of complete confidence on her face.

I'd never seen her look that confident and it blew me away.

9

Amber

"Fuck me," I heard the indrawn breath and spun around.

Honestly, the sentiment was echoing rather loudly up in my brain at the sight of him. But then, it always did.

His gaze travelled up my body slowly until his eyes caught mine and he was looking at me like he saw me as a woman in my own right, not just his best friend's weirdo little sister. It didn't matter that I'd just had a run-in with Dannie and Brent. It didn't matter that Kit was going to remember I was Patrick's baby sister any minute now. It didn't matter I was a virgin who'd never even given herself an orgasm.

The woman who'd looked back at me in the mirror was full of confidence and she looked amazing. Looking at her, I could almost pretend I was the sort of woman Kit liked to have on his arm; tall, leggy, exotic, stunning. I could even almost pretend I had a dirty streak to rival the stories about him.

"Well the navy it is, then," I said, turning back to the mirror. I could still see Kit in the reflection and he didn't look like he was going anywhere.

"Chaos knows his dresses, love," Petra whispered to me, with a wide knowing smile.

I didn't know why that made something in me fall. I knew Kit's reputation probably better than anyone. Patrick was always regaling me with the boys' adventures and I often wondered if he forgot I was his sister rather than just another one of them.

Petra giggled. "I've seen him in here with his clients, love. And nothing but security passes his mind. You're obviously someone very dear to him."

I looked at her and scoffed. "No. I'm just Hawk's little sister."

Her eyes widened. "That's why it feels like I know you."

I looked at her in question and she chuckled.

"You have this familiarity about you. The same smile as Hawk, the same twinkle in your eyes even if they are a far more stunning shade than his." She threw a look back to the sill gob-smacked Kit. "I see his dilemma now."

"What dilemma?" I asked, panicked.

Petra looked into my eyes knowingly. "Love, you don't think it's security on his mind now, do you?"

I looked back at him for a moment, then shook my head. "No," I scoffed. "No. Kit just likes a woman with some skin showing."

Petra leant to my ear. "Then why was he already looking at you like that when you walked in?"

I caught her eye for a moment, not at all believing a thing

she said.

Maybe those fleeting moments I'd been feeling weren't all just me. Maybe I didn't have to convince him I was more than just his best friend's geeky little sister. Maybe he already knew.

But before I could say anything, Kit cleared his throat.

"Right, we should get a move on and let you pack up. Petra, we okay to–?"

"I'll send you everything tomorrow," she finished for him.

He nodded as he cleared his throat. "Thanks."

"Let's get you changed," Petra said with a knowing smile as she led me back to the dressing room. She was laughing by the time I stepped into it.

"What?" I asked.

She shook her head. "Nothing. I've just never seen Chaos speechless before."

I snorted. "He likes to think he's the strong silent type."

"You disagree?"

I looked at her knowingly. "Let's just say that fourteen-year-old Kit Grayson *never* shut up. In that squeaky little, breaking voice of his? It was like he thought the more he talked the quicker it would hurry up and fully break."

"You and I are getting drinks sometime so I can hear more about this," she warned me and I nodded.

"Done."

She left me to get changed, reminding me to be careful about the pins. I don't know what she said to Kit but, when

I walked out, he was both glaring at me and trying not to laugh.

"What?" I asked, pulling my hair back into a messy bun.

"Less than a week and you're already spilling my secrets," he chastised, a sexy half-smirk on his face.

I shrugged, aiming for cute and at least nailing coy. "It's my duty."

He laughed. "I'll allow it. For now." He raised his hand to Petra. "Thanks, again."

Petra smiled. "No problem. Send me a picture of the two of you all dolled up, yeah?"

Kit shook his head as he pulled the door open for me. "Yeah, yeah."

As Kit put his hand to my back, Petra called, "Tank in a tux! And for luck, shirtless!"

Kit huffed a smirk and waved back to her as he walked us out. "Tank won't know what hit him if she gets any ballsier," he muttered.

"She likes him?"

"She certainly likes looking at him."

As we headed towards the Mayhew, I noticed Kit was looking around. I didn't know if he was checking to see if Dannie and Brent were still hanging around of if it was just habit.

"What did you want to do tonight?" he asked eventually.

His tone was nonchalant, like it was something we asked each other all the time. He sounded completely normal asking me that. It wasn't the only thing about the sentence that caught me off-guard.

"Oh. You don't have plans?"

Kit's step faltered as he looked at me. "Do you?"

Something about his manner made me smile. It was almost like he was put out at the idea I'd be doing something not involving him. "Nothing that requires leaving the penthouse," I assured him.

He nodded then paused again at the bottom of the Mayhew's front steps. When he gave me the double-take, I realised what that might have sounded like.

"Study!" I said quickly. "I assumed you'd be busy and I'd study."

He nodded. "Oh. No. Sure." He coughed. "So…I'm not busy. Did you…uh…?"

"Want to hang out?" I finished for him hesitantly.

He nodded again. "That."

"Sure," I said with a smile. "If you can put up with me for a whole night just the two of us."

Kit pulled the Mayhew's door open for me and looked at me as he lay his hand on my arm, just above my wrist like he was about to take my hand again. I wanted to say the look in his eyes said he could handle a night just the two of us and then some. The then some was, of course, of a sexual nature in my fantasy. My breath hitched as Kit and I looked at each other, our bodies probably far too close together. But I wasn't in a hurry to put it to rights.

I saw a heat in his eyes, unrestrained and all about me. I felt his nearness like a tingling warmth against my skin. I was conscious that we were out in public, but I couldn't pull myself away and I wanted to believe he felt the same. His hand slid down towards mine as our bodies swayed closer to each other and…

"Excuse me," a man in a trench coat said as he came up the steps.

Kit and I stepped apart and I swallowed hard.

"Not at all," Kit answered, still holding the door open as the man hurried in.

"Everything all right, Mr Grayson?" came a familiar voice. "Miss Amber?"

I turned to smile at Johnson, somehow sidling towards Kit as I did so.

"Yes. Thank you, Johnson," Kit said with a perfunctory nod. I felt his hand slip into mine, something I saw Johnson noticed. "We're just wondering what to do about dinner. Who's in charge in the restaurant tonight?"

"Franz is on tonight. But if I might offer a suggestion, sir?"

"Of course."

"I always quite like a quiet night in with a bit of pizza, some wine, and a good movie or two." Johnson looked at me knowingly and I inadvertently squeezed Kit's hand as I smiled back at the doorman.

"Sound good?" he asked me.

I nodded. "It does."

"All right. Thank you, Johnson."

We started to head inside when Johnson called out,

"Romanas is *very* good."

Kit nodded back to him as he led me across the foyer to the elevator. Donald caught it for us and we tumbled in with a chuckle.

"Thanks," I said.

"My please, Miss Grace," he replied.

Kit did his thing with the keycard and we rode in silence up to the penthouse. I felt his hand in mine like a flaming beacon. It made me nervous and tense, but at the same time it felt perfectly natural. When the doors opened, a zing of excitement shot through me.

We said good night to Donald and stepped out. After the doors closed, Kit and I bumped into each other in the hallway as he stepped forward at the same time I turned to him. His other hand went to my other arm to catch me and we laughed.

I looked up at him and my heart beat out a mad tango in my chest as my breath caught again.

I couldn't stop thinking about what Petra had said about the way he looked at me, and now I couldn't stop imagining that was exactly how he was looking at me. I knew I shouldn't, but I wanted him to be looking at me like that. And I wanted him to know that's what I wanted.

I tried to think about what any of my romance novel heroines would have done in this situation. I tried to remember how they got the guy to kiss them – because I was far too self-conscious to kiss him first. But then I realised that they were mainly all wallflower virgins with no experience. Just like me. Well, I sure had a type.

Kit licked his lip slowly and the action had me pressing mine together.

I took a deep breath. "Uh… Should we order pizza?" I asked softly.

If I didn't know how to get him to kiss me, then I needed someone to move so I could get my breath back. And I did not trust my legs just then.

He nodded slowly and I entertained the notion he knew that neither of us wanted to move but also that we probably should. "Sure. Got your laptop?"

I gave him a single exaggerated nod as his hand tightened in mine for a split-second, then he was moving away, his fingers trailing through mine as though he was loath to let go. I pulled myself together and hurried over to the dining table for my laptop as Kit went into the kitchen.

"Beer, wine, whiskey, something softer?" he asked, his voice a little huskier than normal.

I picked up my computer and went to the bench. "What do you feel like?"

"I asked you first."

I nodded and I pushed my glasses up. "Yes, then I asked you second."

He huffed a rough laugh. "I feel like starting with a beer."

I smiled up at him as I did a search for Romana Pizza. "Then we'd best start with a beer."

He grinned before turning to the fridge.

I pulled up the ordering system for the pizza and we leant across the bench to meet in the middle and decide what we wanted. There was a lot of laughing and quite a few shared smiles. As we headed to the lounge to pick a movie, I felt the most at ease I'd ever felt with Kit. Sure I was still apparently mush on the inside around him, but it was like all the tension had left our relationship and all we were left with were two people who'd known each other forever.

"What is it with you and Pat having uncomfortable couches?" I grumbled as I tried to get comfortable.

He paused in his movie search to look at me. "What do you mean?"

"I mean, what is your obsession with looking like a homemaker catalogue?"

Kit looked around the living room. "I've never thought about it. We just got a decorator in."

I rolled my eyes at him. "Of course, you did."

He looked at me and there went that full smile. "What?"

My eyes scanned the room. "It's so…unliveable…"

"All right," he chuckled. "You can have re-decorating power, then."

"First thing that's going is this God-awful couch."

"You know, no one has ever complained about my couch before."

"Has anyone ever sat on your couch before?"

"Yes."

"Other than the team?"

He paused, then nodded. "Yes."

"They were probably too busy thinking about your cock," I heard myself say, then looked at him in what felt like a combination of shock and panic. "Uh…" I started, not sure where I was going with that or how I was going to backpedal. "Not that I'm thinking…" I winced. "Have thought…about…your…" *Shut up, Amber!* I cleared my throat and nodded, refusing to look at him. "Yep."

Kit snorted. "Okay. Good to know."

I looked at him sideways and felt myself fighting a smile. Completely unable to help myself, my eyes dropped to his crotch. Not that I could see much because he was leaning forward on his knees. I could imagine with the best of them, though. By the time my eyes slid back to his face, he was smirking around the top of his beer bottle.

"What?" I asked, feeling my cheeks heat.

He shrugged as he swallowed, sat back and dropped his hand with the beer bottle into his lap. "Just wondering how that not thinking about…it thing is going for you."

Well that new pose wasn't helping.

I laughed as I looked away. "Virgin is not synonymous with prude, Christopher," I told him.

"Oh, really? Colour me intrigued."

I shot him a quick smile, then dropped back onto the couch and leant towards him. "A girl can still daydream without having first-hand experience."

"Can she?"

"What?" I scoffed. "Like you can't?"

His eyes scanned my body like a hot caress. He looked

around for a moment then leant towards me like he was going to share a secret with me. I tilted closer to him. "I've always been more a jump first, ask questions later kind of guy." His voice slid over me tantalisingly and I firmly believed that had been his intention.

If the intercom hadn't buzzed, I totally would have told him he could go right on and jump me. But, when we sat back down with the pizza, it was like we both knew we'd come close to crossing a line and we kept to our sides of the couch. Mostly.

10
Kit

Ugh. I had to be more fucking careful. I'd lost count of the times I'd almost kissed her now.

The whole night before had been one near miss after another. I just hadn't been able to stop myself reaching for her. I wanted to hold her, to touch her, to kiss her. And I was having a hard – pun intended – time telling myself to leave off because she didn't feel the same. It was getting more difficult to stoically believe that her eyes didn't linger on me, that desire didn't cross her face as she'd unsubtly looked at my crotch, or that the fact she was my best mate's little sister was a strong enough excuse to behave.

We'd stayed up late, eating and drinking and watching movies. We'd laughed and flirted like teenagers dating. It had been foreign and familiar all at once – like I knew this Amber even if I'd never seen her before. She was totally unguarded with me and I'd fucking loved it.

Eventually, we'd dragged ourselves to our own beds and I'd only fallen asleep after I'd relieved a modicum of my tension. By the time I'd woken up again, it was back with reinforcements. Not that there was time to do anything about it because, just as I decided a shower and a wank would do me good, the intercom buzzer was sounding.

I hauled myself out of bed, threw on some tracksuit pants and went out to answer it.

"Yes?"

"I have the team from Grace Grayson here to see you, sir," I heard Donald's voice.

"Oi, oi!" came Rollie's voice.

"Open up, mate!" I heard Hawk chuckle.

I threw a look towards Amber's room, guilt and panic flooding me momentarily. But what did I have to be guilty about? I cleared my throat before I hit the intercom button again. "Come on up then, you wankers."

I hit the accept button so the doors would open when the lift got to the floor.

While I waited for them, I started on coffee. I didn't miss the fact that I started Amber's first, but I wasn't going to make a big thing of it.

"I have boxes. So many boxes," I heard Tank's deep rumbling chuckle.

"And I've got the truck," Hawk boomed in his announcer's voice.

"And I have…the diplomatic flags," Rollie said, flourishing them as he appeared in front of me.

"You have the…?" I grabbed his wrist so he stopped moving it around. "Where the fuck did you get those?"

Rollie beamed. "The ambassador's wife nicked me a pair

and said I should use them…" He winked, "at my discretion." His wrist got free and he waved the flags again. "I thought they'd help us with parking."

"She probably expected you to use them next time you…parked in her," Hawk laughed as he went to companionably kick Rollie in the arse.

"Ew, Pat," Amber said as she walked out from the other side of the apartment.

I looked up quickly, but I didn't know what I expected to find; it was like something had changed between us and I felt like everyone was going to see it before I even knew what it was. She was smiling at the boys and, when she looked at me for a moment, there was something palpable in her humoured glance. I could feel the tension between her and me from across the room. The kind that had me wanting to go over to her and kiss her, even in front of my team and her big brother. I'd never felt *that* sort of tension between us before and I couldn't work out what it meant going forward.

"And this must be the lovely Amber?" Rollie asked her, presumably not sensing anything was off.

"It is," she replied with a nod as she took everyone in.

"Right, Bert," Hawk said. "You know Nico. This is Rollie and Tank."

I watched her give a small wave and started passing out the coffees in their convenient travel mugs.

"Hi, guys. Nice to meet you."

"Finally," Tank rumbled.

"Finally," Amber agreed.

"We ready for this?" Rollie asked.

She nodded and her smile widened. "Yes. Thank you so much for helping, guys."

All the boys stopped whatever lack of anything they were doing and looked at her.

"Amber," Tank said with a soft chastise. "We're family."

"Family sticks together," Nico added solemnly.

"Family fucks up the fuckers who hurt you!" Rollie added a little more vehemently.

"Rollie!" we all yelled and he turned around with his most innocent grin on his face.

Sweet, gorgeous Amber went over to hug Rollie. "Thank you anyway," she laughed.

Rollie pointed at her back and smiled widely at us. "Someone appreciates me."

Amber let go of him and shook her head as Tank told him, "Only because she didn't have to live in a tent with your bare arse for two months."

"The first time," Hawk reminded us. "You two ready to go?"

I nodded. "Let me grab a shirt."

"Good idea, genius," Hawk snickered, then looked at his sister. "You got your keys, Bert?"

She blinked and finally took her eyes off me and patted her pockets. "What? Keys. Yes."

Hawk nodded. "Great, let's do this."

134

"I'll get the truck to the front door," Rollie said, brandishing his flags.

"What?" Amber asked.

I went to get a shirt as I heard Hawk say, "Rollie fancies himself a foreign ambassador."

"I could be. They don't know I'm not."

"That's still some shady shit," Tank said disapprovingly, but he'd long since tried to stop what he couldn't control.

"Are we doing this, or what?" I said as I came out, flicking the hood of my tank top back.

Amber nodded, looking like she was forcing the courage. "Sure. Five big, strong boys behind me. I can do this."

"Yes. You can," Nico said warmly and there was a little touch of jealousy in me, particularly at the way she smiled back at him.

To make myself feel better, I was incredibly mature and grown up and reminded myself that Nico couldn't have her either.

The six of us squashed into the lift.

"Morning, Mr Grayson. Miss Grace," Donald said, crushed in the corner.

"Morning, Don," I replied, momentarily distracted as my hand brushed Amber's. I felt a zing of electricity between us like an electric shock, but so much sweeter.

I looked at her quickly and saw she was looking at me, too. My heart pounded in my chest and I was sure the others were going to be able to tell. I cleared my throat and moved as far away from her as the cramped lift allowed.

"Rollie, hit the fucking button, will you?" I snapped.

"Call me Buzz," he said as he hit the button for the carpark.

We all turned to look at him. "What? Why?" we all asked independently.

"Because today I'm a moving guy. Not a security guy."

I wasn't the only one to sigh and mutter something less than complimentary about him and his 'humour'. But soon the lift was filled with their overlapping chatter and Hawk's and Rollie's laughter. I snuck a look at Amber and saw that she was a little hunched in on herself. She pushed her glasses up and took a deep breath.

I felt my hand reach out to her even though I know I shouldn't. I shouldn't have the night before and I definitely shouldn't when her brother was in the lift with us.

"You okay?" I asked quietly.

"I will be." I felt her squeeze my hand gently. "Thanks."

We looked at each other and I wanted to be anywhere but a lift full of the boys, let alone her older brother. Looking at her, it was like my heart restarted or some sappy shit. I wanted to tell her. I wanted to be worth her. But I couldn't. And I wasn't.

The lift came to a stop and Amber and I separated hastily.

Rollie led the way to the truck, skipping and waving his flags around like a total twat. But it got a laugh out of Amber, which I was certain had been the aim. The Grace

Grayson team might have been toughened men of action, but we were also pretty perceptive. Bets were, the whole lift had noticed her trepidation.

We bundled into the truck. Hawk, Rollie and Amber in the cab and Nico, Tank and me in the back. Technically illegal, but who was going to see us? Hawk was a total dick as usual and had a brilliant time accelerating and braking really hard so we were thrown around. It was enough to even get a rise out of the usually level-headed Tank.

He banged on the front of the compartment. "I will end you!" he shouted.

Whether Hawk had heard him or we'd exited the carpark, the ride was smoother. For the few short minutes it took to get to the front of Amber's old building. After Hawk let us out of the back – I punched him for good measure but he just laughed – and Rollie was done with his flags, Tank and I got out the boxes. I watched as Hawk fussed over his baby sister as she hovered at the front door.

Rollie was the first one in with an, "I'll get the elevator!"

Amber snapped herself out of whatever was in her head to follow him. "We're not all fitting in that thing and I solidly refuse."

The rest of us followed her, but we all paused outside the lift as she started up the stairs.

"I'm serious," she said. "You want whiplash and a near-death experience, be my guest."

"I'm not scared," Rollie decided, pressing the call button.

"I personally quite like my skin where it is," Nico said. "I'mma take the stairs with Amber."

She grinned and led the way.

"What floor?" Rollie called.

"Four," Amber replied.

"Race you!" Rollie yelled.

Amber laughed as the rest of us followed her up the stairs.

She paused at the lift and chuckled to herself. "He might be a while."

She went over to a door, blew out a heavy breath, nodded, and put her key in.

She pushed open the door and looked in cautiously. There was nothing from inside. No exclamation of surprise she was there. No greeting. Just silence. Maybe we should have said something when we'd run into Dannie the night before, but I honestly hadn't thought of it.

"All good?" Hawk whispered.

Amber nodded and edged her way in. "Yeah. All good."

The four of us bustled in behind her.

"How do you want to do this?" Nico asked as Tank started unfolding the boxes.

Amber sighed and shrugged. "I don't know. There's a bunch of stuff just around, plus my room…"

"Why don't a couple of us take your room?" Hawk asked. "You can direct the rest of us out here."

"What about Rollie?" Tank asked.

"Fucker can ferry boxes when he finally shows up,"

Hawk said.

"I told him the elevator sucked," Amber said. She sighed again as she looked around. "But, yeah. Okay. Sounds like a plan."

"Tank, help me with her room?" Hawk asked.

"You remember which one it is?" Amber looked at him.

He gave a nod. "Just put everything we find in boxes?"

"That's the plan."

Hawk and Tank took a couple of boxes down a corridor off the main living space. It wasn't big, but it was homely. Far more homely than the penthouse would ever be, I was sure. There was evidence of life lived here. The best thing going for the penthouse was that Amber left all her study stuff spread around. At the very least, the penthouse was an exclusive university study hall. But I had given Amber permission to re-decorate, so who knew what it would look like soon.

"All right, tell us what to pack," Nico said.

Amber breathed out like she was thinking. She nodded, then headed for the kitchen. "Okay."

Tank had remembered to bring some newspaper so we could wrap up all the breakables before putting them away. Amber's assertive streak shone as she passed us things to wrap, pointed at stuff for us to grab, or handed us something to put in a box. It was a weirdly efficient system.

When Rollie eventually arrived – not really that long after – he ran into Dannie and the dickweed in the hallway on his way back out with a box.

"Excuse me," I heard Dannie's voice. "Who are you and why are you in my apartment?"

Amber caught my eye and I could see she wasn't looking forward to this confrontation. I stepped forward and Dannie's eyes snapped to me.

"Chaos?" she said sweetly, Brent glowering behind her. "What are you doing here?"

"We're helping Amber pack up her stuff."

"You mean she's *moving in* with you?" Brent asked, taking a step forward.

There was enough challenge in him that I was pretty sure he knew he'd royally cocked up. He'd fucked the wrong girl and he'd lost the right one. Well, Amber wasn't his and I wasn't giving him a chance to even try to win her back. Even if no one else in the room noticed how possessive I suddenly felt, Brent did.

"Okay," Hawk's voice broke obliviously through the silent tension in the room. "You'll be super proud of me. I did *not* bare butt fart on Dannie…is standing right there…" he petered off.

"So kind of you to not give me pink eye, Patrick," she said to him.

But Hawk was done being civil to this little shit – he'd never liked her. "It is the least of what you deserve after you stole Bert's boyfriend, you slag."

Dannie acted shocked. "I didn't steal anyone. Brent wanted to be with me."

I smirked as I stepped up beside Hawk. It was the two of

us against the two of them. "You regretting that easy lay now, mate?" I asked him cavalierly.

"I don't have to explain myself to men with children's names," Brent said haughtily.

I nodded. "You might be right there. But at least be man enough to admit you fucked up. An apology is surely not beyond a man as…mature as you."

"You intimidated by the ex?" Brent tried.

All five Grace Grayson boys laughed. Mine had less humour in it than it should have.

"Intimidated? No, mate," I said, taking another step towards him. "Little boys not man enough to keep an amazing young woman are nothing to me."

"I see you're fine hiding behind these buffoons, Amber…" Dannie said.

Amber walked forward to stand between us all. "I'm not hiding. I'm just getting on with my life. Something I think the two of you should probably do."

Dannie looped her arm in Brent's. "We *are* dating, you know."

Amber looked them over. "How nice. You two deserve each other." She turned on her heel and started back to the kitchen.

Brent pulled his arm out from Dannie's and went to follow her. My hand rose from years of practise to stop him. He glared at me but didn't fight me. "Amber!" he pleaded. "Come on. Can we at least talk about this?"

"Brent?" Dannie cried, frowning at his back.

"There's nothing to talk about," Amber said, barely looking up from the mug she was wrapping.

"There is. Let me explain. Apologise properly. Please. I love you."

The whole room went deadly still. Amber lowered her hands, the cup still half-wrapped in it, and looked at him over the rims of her glasses.

"You loved me, but you couldn't go a few months without sex for me?"

He shrugged wildly. "It was a mistake. An accident."

"Brent, closing your hand in the door is a mistake. That's an accident–"

"But I love you."

"And you think that makes it all better? Three words don't excuse cheating, Brent."

"Don't you love me?"

I felt like I was at the tennis. Heads swivelled one side to the other to see what the next person would say.

"No," Amber said simply.

"What? Not at all?"

Amber shrugged gently. "Nope."

"Of course, she'd say that now," Dannie scoffed.

Amber looked totally calm, totally confident, she was in charge here. "You believe whatever you want to. I know my truth and that is, quite frankly, all that matters. What the two of you think of me is no longer my problem."

Brent sniffed. "So, that's it? It's over?"

Amber laughed, but it was humourless. "It was over

when I found you under my best friend."

"Amber…babe–"

I stepped closer to him. "You heard her," I growled.

"Kit, leave him be," Amber told me. "I'll be done here soon, Dannie. I'll leave the key when I lock up."

"You're kicking me out of my own apartment?"

"You're welcome to stay. Just don't get in the boys' way."

Dannie looked like she was going to argue. For about five seconds. She then stormed out. Brent had no choice but to follow her, what with not only me but Hawk scowling at him like looks could kill. As soon as they were in the hallway, they started arguing.

"You love her?"

"What do you want me to say?"

"Not that you love her!"

"It was always her."

"It wasn't her when you had your dick in me."

"You're a mistake, Dannie!"

"Well…" Rollie chuckled awkwardly as he pushed the door closed exaggeratedly. "Wasn't that fun?"

"You okay, Bert?" Hawk asked.

She nodded, a little shaky but still confident. "Yeah. I'm okay."

"For real?"

She smiled at him. "For real."

He nodded. "Okay. Let's be here for as little time as possible."

We finished packing up all of Amber's stuff and loaded it in the truck. We didn't see Dannie or Brent again, but Amber did really seem okay. All I wanted was to console her, to wrap my arms around her and make sure she was okay. But that wasn't something we did and I was going to keep reminding myself of that.

The guys helped us get the boxes and furniture loaded up in the lift at the Mayhew, while Donald held the doors open for us – it took a good few trips. I knew what this looked like to him and I knew what gossip was going to be spread around the rest of the staff as soon as his shift ended. But I didn't care. As long as Amber was safe, I didn't care.

"Fuck me, that was a lot of shit, Bert," Hawk sighed after all her belongings were in the penthouse as he helped himself to a beer out of my fridge.

"I'm a collector," was her defence.

"Chaos is gonna need to let you put some of it out here. It's not all fitting in your room."

I'd spoken to Hawk about the living arrangements. I'd told him Amber was planning to live with me until she finished studying at least. He'd been fine with it. But he wouldn't have if he knew what thoughts my traitorous head was entertaining about her.

I looked to Amber and saw she was looking at me. Too many things passed between us unsaid. I felt every single one to the depths of my soul. I wanted to take all her hurt away and make sure it never came near her again. I wanted to make sure she never felt small or used ever again. Now

I'd seen so much of it, I couldn't bare for her to ever doubt her confidence again.

"Of…of course," I finally said. "Re-decorating power and all. Unpack whatever wherever. Make yourself at home."

Rollie chuckled as Hawk passed him another of my beers. "Careful, mate. You might end up with panties on the chandeliers."

"Oh, so like your place then?" I replied, feeling like I was forcing the normality, but it was better than nothing.

We all fell into a relaxed conversation as we all shared a couple of beers. The guys only stayed for an hour or so, then they headed off for places to be, jobs or 'dates' and the like.

"So…" Amber said as she picked up the beer bottles and took them to the kitchen. "Thanks again for all your help today."

I shook my head. "No problem." I drummed my hands on the kitchen counter, totally at a loss for words and feeling like a teenage boy in the first awkward throes of my first crush.

"Did you–" I asked as she said, "Were we–"

"You go," she said with a shy smile.

I shook my head. "No. After you."

She smiled as she looked down. "I was just thinking we could set the console up. I've still got *Street Fighter*…" Her eyes rose and there was a challenge in them.

This was a challenge I could answer. I smirked. "You think you can beat me?" I chuckled.

She shrugged. "I've had *a lot* of time to practise…"

"I'll believe it when I see it."

She grinned warmly, then jogged off to one of the boxes. I got another couple of beers out while she set it up and did not keep my eyes off her arse in any way.

We dropped onto the couch, our thighs bumping together but neither of us moving away. Strictly speaking, we were too close. I wasn't sure I trusted myself at that distance and the last thing she needed after such a harrowing day was me being all…vibe-y.

But she didn't seem to care. And, truth be told, she was giving off some vibes of her own.

She fair and square beat me in the first two games, but I was beating her steadily for the third. Half her health was gone and I was gearing up for my uber move. Amber, obviously, wasn't having any of it.

Her shoulder nudged mine and she put her hand over my controller.

"Interference!" I called and she laughed.

"No! No! No!" she giggled as she held her controller as far away from me as possible and uber moved the shit out of my fighter.

"Total interference, ref," I said as I tried to reach for her controls with my longer arms.

She shook her head as she turned to me and our noses bumped.

There was this look in her eyes that screamed at me to kiss the girl, that the girl wanted me to kiss her. Her chest rose and fell against me rapidly. Every nerve in my body was on alert to her. My heart skipped a beat and I suddenly forgot why this whole thing was a bad idea.

My arm was on the back of the couch behind her, the other one stretched for her controller. Almost as one, our stretched arms dropped together. I trailed my fingers over her shoulder and felt her hand on my leg. I dipped my face towards her slightly, touching my forehead to hers for a moment. She inhaled quickly, but then I felt her reaching up towards me.

At the exact moment our lips met, "K.O.," came the call and I pulled away from her and looked at the TV.

I spluttered a laugh to see her fighter victorious onscreen. I looked back at Amber in disbelief. She had her hand over her mouth and her eyes were full of cheeky humour.

"Did you actually just…?" I asked, sparing a quick glance to the controller still in her hand.

She shook her head wildly. "No," came her muffled reply. She held both hands up innocently, looking both apologetic and like she was about to burst into laughter. "No. That was a total accident. I swear."

My eyebrow rose. "Sure it was."

"No," she laughed. "I promise it was."

"I demand a rematch, Amber Grace."

She tried to draw herself up intimidatingly. "Game on, Christopher."

As we into battle, we laughed and there was no mention made of the almost-kiss for the rest of the night. I wasn't sure if I was glad about that or not.

147

11
Amber

I took my time waking up on Sunday morning, feeling better than I had in a long time. I felt like, after taking a million steps backwards, I was finally moving on with my life.

Sure, I'd lost basically my only two real friends and my boyfriend in one fell swoop, left most of my belongings behind and found myself living with my walking wet dream. But my life was my own again, my stuff was with me, and I could actually hold a conversation with Kit without making a total twat out of myself.

I squealed in disbelief and covered my face as I remembered that, for one brief moment, it had been even better because my lips had brushed his. I felt elated and terrified at the knowledge that I wasn't the only one thinking things that probably shouldn't be thought. I wasn't the only one thinking about kissing instead of talking, the only one stealing glances. I wasn't making up the sizzle. I just didn't know how to take it from a brush of the lips to a kiss to make me forget my own name.

I was also shit scared of what would happen after the

148

kiss. And I simultaneously didn't care at all as long as I got one taste of him.

My head was a hot mess and I couldn't wipe the ridiculous smile off my face.

"I need a heavy dose of reality and a larger dose of caffeine," I muttered to myself as I pulled on my glasses and dragged myself out of bed like the risen undead.

I padded out to the living area and blinked to find Kit already up. He was wearing knee-length shorts and a hooded tank top both in tracksuit material. His feet were bare and his hair was still sticking up like he hadn't been up for long or, like me, he didn't really care what he looked like.

"Morning," I yawned as I slouched over to the breakfast bar.

"Morning. Coffee?"

"Ugh, please," I mumbled, lying my head on my arms and watching him.

He shot me a look over his shoulder and grinned. "How were you feeling about going over some self-defence stuff this morning?" he asked.

I sighed. "Uh…lazy."

"I thought so."

"How detrimental to my health would it be if I took a pass on that?"

He turned and leant on the bench so our noses were almost touching. An electric zing shot through me and I wriggled my nose. Kit looked me over and his smile was softer.

"Depends on if you're running away or okay, I guess."

I tilted my head to the other side. "Would you believe me if I said okay?"

His look was more searching this time, like he could actually see into my soul or something. "I would."

I nodded. "Then I'm saved from exercise today?"

He huffed a laugh as he stood up. "Sure. Why not."

I smiled as I spun myself on the stool. "Okay. Good."

"Do you need to study?"

I looked at all my stuff on the table. "How much are we planning on drinking tonight?" I countered.

He appeared beside me and rested against the bench. "Mondays are usually pretty quiet for us. Could be a lot."

I looked at him, his muscles and his ink tantalising me, his hands all strong but gentle as they held his mug. If I let him start teaching me self-defence then he'd probably have to put them all over me.

Because that was a good idea. My already raging libido needed there to be excessive skin-on-skin contact.

"I'd best get to studying then."

He nodded. "All right. I'll leave you to it."

It was not what I wanted, but it was the sensible thing to do. Also, I hadn't done any work the day before and I had a feeling I wouldn't get any done the next day either. So I took my coffee from him, relishing the way my skin tingled as our fingers touched, and went to my pile of mess on his table.

For the first few minutes, my eyes kept lifting and following him as he moved around doing whatever it was he did. But the next thing I realised was him walking into his room and telling me we'd have to leave soon and my dress was on the corner of the table. I was used to getting lost in my work to avoid the real world, but even that was impressive.

I hurriedly packed up, had the quickest shower of my life, and pulled on the dress Petra had sent up for me. I felt ever so slightly out of my element but, when I caught a look at myself in the mirror, all doubts were gone. Just like Friday, when I saw myself in that dress, I looked like a freaking queen, a proper adult woman and I felt amazing.

"Watch out, world," I murmured as I took one last look at my arse, grabbed up my phone and a coat and hurried out.

Kit appeared at his bedroom door and…

"Damn," I whispered.

Kit was wearing a black tuxedo with white shirt and black tie. He took my damn breath away. He was like your renaissance romance all wrapped up in a delicious package. I was thinking heavily of giving that McLean's thing a miss and to try that masturbation thing one more time. I was pretty sure I'd get it this time.

But better than the way Kit looked was the way he was looking at me.

Oh, I was going to sear this memory into my brain for life.

As I walked over to him, he looked me over like I was

anything other than his best friend's little sister, like I was anything other than a geek who didn't know what she was doing – either in the bedroom or in life. I could feel the heels making my hips sway more than usual and I was going to just soak up the adoration in his eyes.

We met in the middle of the room, our eyes pinned to each other.

It was one of those moments you were supposed to kiss. One of those moments you summed up your whole range of emotions in a single physical action. I wanted it. Badly. Kit made me feel things – want things – I'd thought I was okay without. He made me want to throw caution to the wind, to tell Patrick I could do what I wanted. But I knew what me kissing him would do to his friendship with my brother, and I wasn't so far gone to do that to either of them no matter how much I wanted to.

Kit's eyes never left mine as he took my coat from my hands and wrapped it around me with a smile.

"You ready?" he asked.

I nodded.

"You okay to walk?"

McLean's was on the same street as Petra's and the Mayhew so I figured I could suffer the short-term wrath of the high heeled shoe. I didn't wear them often. Actually, I couldn't remember the last time I had worn them. But Farrah and Dannie had always told me I was a natural on them and they were completely disgusted at that.

I nodded again. "Yeah, all good."

His hand went to my back as we walked to the elevator, then again as we walked through the foyer and out the Mayhew's front door with a nod to Johnson.

Kit's hand trailed along my back and paused near my hand. Finally, he offered me his elbow and I took it, wondering what on Earth we must look like. Then I remembered I was dressed just as well as him and realised we would have looked like any normal couple heading out to dinner.

Not that we were a couple, I had to remind myself.

This stretch of road was a strange one. It had a mix of uptown and downtown; rich and barely getting by. Although Dannie's building was one of the last of what we called the cheapo apartments and, even then, they were only cheap when you weren't doing it alone.

Kit slid his arm from mine as he reached to open a door for me and I realised we'd made it to McLean's. He gave me a warm smile and I returned it before he stepped forward. He held the door open for me as I followed, then his hand went to the small of my back and I fought off the pleasant shiver down my spine.

It was easy to pick out the Grace Grayson boys, sitting in a back corner of the restaurant. And that wasn't just because I'd seen Patrick – not many tables had four huge guys sitting around it with two spare chairs.

"Christopher," a warm voice said and I pulled my eyes off Patrick waving his hands around to find a suave older gentleman in a black suit.

"McLean. Thanks for fitting us in at such short notice," Kit said as he shook the man's hand.

McLean beamed. "Nonsense. You know Grace Grayson are some of my best customers."

"We certainly like our food and drink. This is Amber Grace," he said as he helped me out of my coat.

McLean turned that smile on me. "Patrick's sister, I'll wager?"

I nodded, holding my hand out. But instead of shaking it, he kissed the back of it lightly.

"Uh, yes."

He took my coat and Kit's, then pointed to our table. "Wonderful to meet you. The others have drinks already. We'll come by shortly to take your orders."

Kit smiled. "Thanks."

The hand on my back pressed forward and I let him show me over to our table.

"Chaos!" Rollie cried as we got closer.

But my eyes had fallen on Patrick who was looking me over with his mouth agape. "Bert!" he breathed. "You look… Wow. You look really wow," he said as he helped me into a chair.

Tank – also known as Gavin Hamilton – was just as big as I'd imagined. He had dark hair and light brown eyes that sparkled with humour. I could imagine he'd be a scary guy when he wanted but, between helping me pack up my stuff the day before and now, I hadn't seen any of that.

Rollie – who had been christened Ryder Andrews – was

the smallest of the bunch and he looked as much the mischief maker as I'd been led to believe, and he'd more than lived up to his reputation since I'd met him. His auburn hair was longer than most, but shorter than Nico's, and he had green eyes that did more than hint at the trouble his smirk suggested.

Nico had lost some of his charm in his three-piece suit, but it also added a whole new level of hot to him. Unlike the others, he looked the most uncomfortable but he smiled when I looked at him and gave a little wave.

Rollie grinned as he poured me a glass. "So, we made sure there was plenty of champagne in advance–"

"We can't call it champagne unless it's from Champagne," Tank interrupted, his glass looking comically small in his big hand.

Patrick picked up the bottle Rollie wasn't dishing out and looked at the label. "Champagne. France. So there."

I huffed a laugh but was unfortunately taking a sip at the time and splashed my glasses. As I took them off to clean them, the boys kept talking around me.

"Remind me," Rollie said, passing Kit a glass. "Champagne had that gorgeous little blonde?"

Nico looked thoroughly unimpressed as he crossed his arms. "I think you'll have to be more specific about the particular blonde."

"That can wait," Tank said, leaning in and holding up his glass. "First, we need to make a toast to Amber."

"Yes!" Rollie grinned, holding up his glass as well, and

the rest followed suit.

Patrick cleared his throat as though he was about to make some terribly important speech. "To kickarse first draft chapters."

"To letting your geek flag fly," Nico added sombrely, although there was a touch of a smile in his eyes.

"To being with loved ones," Tank said.

"To beating the shit out of people who hurt you," was Rollie's contribution, which was met with a combination of humour and reprimand.

"To finally adding Amber to the family," Kit finished up, more sincerity in his tone and his eyes than I deserved.

I looked around at them all, feeling one of those warm happy bubbles grow in my chest. It was hard to believe that Patrick and Kit and their friends had put everything aside to take me out to dinner. And by the looks on all their faces, they weren't even regretting it.

"Thanks for having me," I answered.

"Well, now you and Chaos don't hate each other, it was about time," Patrick said with a warm smile.

I didn't feel the need to correct him, knowing I'd probably just end up mumbling and blushing like an idiot. So, I just let them toast me.

We all raised our glasses for a moment, then drank.

The boys were all big and boisterous in their own ways and I sat and watched their interactions avidly the way I hadn't been able to do much the day before. Kit and Nico were by far the quietest of them. Nico let very little out but a small smile or snort of laughter now and then, and Kit even less. With both of them, you could see the humour behind their eyes but it was like they couldn't let themselves completely relax even among their closest friends.

"All right. So, I want gossip," Rollie announced, leaning for the champagne bottle again and staring right at me.

"Gossip?" I clarified.

He nodded and pointed at Patrick and Kit with the bottle before pouring more drinks for that side of the table. "Gossip. These two as gangly teens. Awkward haircuts. Girls who turned them down. I want gossip."

I looked between Patrick and Kit, trying to fight a smile. "Gossip?"

"Amber…" Kit said, a teasing warning in his voice.

"Nah. We're right, mate," Patrick said, all bluster. "We didn't do gangly or awkward."

Kit nodded and I felt his knee bump mine as he shifted in his seat. "You're so right," he said as we caught each other's eye.

I didn't let the moment distract me.

"Yeah, but I remember the two of you fighting over Missy Fletcher in Year Nine," I said.

All eyes turned to me, most in interest, four in horror.

"Who won?" Rollie asked.

"My money's on Chaos," Tank said quickly.

"Nah. Hawk for sure," Rollie said. "Nico?"

Nico shook his head slowly, his arms crossed over his chest. "No comment."

"What? Too scared to bet on the bosses?"

The corner of Nico's lips rose in the smallest of smirks, but his eyes shone behind his glasses. "Want to tell him?"

I grinned, but Patrick interrupted me with a, "Bert…"

"Neither of them won," I told the table, ignoring the disgruntled sighs on either side of me. "She turned them both down for the captain of the chess team."

Tank snorted champagne out of his nose, Rollie's mouth dropped open and his eyes went wide, and Nico looked smugly satisfied.

"What?" Patrick asked and I felt him shrug. "Girl was a grade-A nerd."

"We didn't speak nerd at fourteen," Kit added, his voice smooth.

"Oh, and you do now?" Nico scoffed.

"How much do you need to get them in bed?" Patrick chuckled and I smacked him.

"It's not like we're a different species. Thank you," I huffed.

"Oh!" Rollie laughed. "Baby Grace has got sass."

"Like you wouldn't believe, man," Kit chuckled as he tipped his glass to his lips.

"It's not like you were any better as a teenager," Patrick huffed to me.

I indicated the table. "Tell them anything you want, Pat. I promise you, you don't know the most embarrassing stories."

Tank erupted in deep laughter as Rollie said, "And I

doubt he wants to know them."

Patrick wouldn't be dissuaded and stories flowed back and forth about the Graces and Kit when we were younger. Pat was horrified at some of the things I remembered, where Kit seemed happy to own his embarrassments. While I was pretty sure there wasn't a single thing that would be more embarrassing than the way I usually was around Kit. Which didn't seem to be a problem anymore…

Even when Kit's arm brushed mine or I unthinkingly put my hand on his arm while I said something, I didn't feel as awkward as usual. I felt like I was holding my own. In public and everything. I didn't know if it was the other boys, or the setting, the dress, or the way he'd reacted to it, but I felt good. Really good. Better even than when I'd woken up.

When Kit's elbow brushed passed me while we were eating, I turned and gave him a small smile and a nudge back. I blamed the amount of champagne I'd had. But all he did was give me a little smirk in return and went back to whatever he was saying to Tank.

But…that little smirk. For the split second he'd given me that smirk, I'd felt something. It was something that had been building the last few days. It made my heart beat wildly in my chest. It made my smile widen. It felt like there really was something more there. Something I wasn't imagining and something even Patrick couldn't stand in the way of.

After we finished eating, Tank stood up and bowed to me, extending his hand gracefully. "Might I have this dance,

Miss Grace?" he asked.

I smiled. "You may, Mr Hamilton," I replied.

I let him pull me to standing and found my footing steadier than I'd been expecting. My eyes found Kit's as I stood and a look passed between us that felt more charged than usual, felt more possessive. I bit my lip against the nervous grin that was trying to escape and pushed my glasses up my nose. As Tank led me to the dance floor, I was almost sure that I felt Kit's finger trail along my leg and almost catch my fingers. But when I looked back at him, there was no indication he'd done anything of the sort.

"I'm glad Hawk decided to finally let us meet you," Tank said with a smile as he took my hand gently in his.

"Me too. I think before with…" I'd been about to blurt out about me and Kit not getting on, but I didn't seem to need to finish what I was saying as Tank nodded.

"It's no great secret that you and Chaos have never…seen eye to eye." A deep chuckle rumbled through his broad chest and I was even more convinced that Tank was the perfect nickname for him. But with a smile on his face and laughter in those light brown eyes, there was nothing remotely scary about him.

"Ah…that's one way of putting it."

Tank's eyebrows shot up. "You'd put it a different way?"

I shrugged coyly. "No. No. That works." I certainly wasn't about to tell him the real reason I'd never been able to look at or talk to Kit. "We're different people I guess."

Tank barked a short laugh. "That's putting it mildly. But Chaos loves you like his own sister."

My stomach flip-flopped and my eyes slid to Kit. Suddenly I was second-guessing everything that had happened between us. Of course, it could be read as Kit just being kind to his best friend's little sister. That was probably all it was and the rest was my horny imagination running away with me.

In an effort to push the pang of disappointment down, I smiled and said, "And he's yet another big brother I never wanted."

"And you've just got yourself three more," Tank said and my smile was anything but forced.

Tank and I danced and chatted a while longer, then Rollie came and decided it was his turn to woo the fair maiden – his words.

"So how goes our first Champers Day?" Rollie asked me as he twirled me around expertly.

I grinned. "Very well."

"We're doing it right? Tank tried Googling it, but couldn't find anything."

I snorted. "Ah. No. It was a thing my friends and I made up. Like girls' night, but for special occasions. Graduations, passing exams, getting a job, or…" I paused.

"What?"

"Losing our virginity…" I laughed and he grinned warmly.

"Oh yeah?"

I nodded. "Yes."

"Well, I for one am honoured you let us share this one with you."

I felt a warm and fuzzy inside at his tone, but a familial one. "I'm glad I did, Ryder."

He wrinkled his nose. "God, it's been forever since anyone called me that," he chuckled.

"Why *do* they call you Rollie?" I asked him.

"Ah." He smirked. "Most of us got into the habit of smoking while we were deployed. The least mind-impairing stress-relief we'd allow ourselves–"

"You mean weed?" I hissed.

He laughed. "No. Just tobacco. But I've always preferred rollies, preferably unfiltered. The name stuck."

"You still smoke?"

He shrugged. "Not often. The rest of the guys managed to quit all right. Nico replaced nicotine with the dark web or something. Tank replaced it with a punching bag. And Hawk and Chaos…" He stopped almost guiltily and I had an idea where this was going.

"Sex."

He nodded. "Pretty much."

I smiled. "I guess there are worse vices?"

He shrugged. "It could definitely be worse."

Talk turned to lighter things after that. And after a while, Nico came to butt in muttering, "They'll make me at some point anyway."

"You don't want to dance with me?" I joked as he put

his hand on my waist.

He shook his head. "I didn't say that. I just don't like dancing. It's nothing against you. But since this is Amber Appreciation Champers Day, I am beholden to dance with you. So, I thought I'd get it over with."

I smirked. "And how long is an acceptable amount of time to do so?"

He looked down for a moment. "Actually, now I'm here, I don't mind I so much."

"Is that because I manage to make you look good?"

He laughed. "Yeah. Probably."

His laughter was infectious and I couldn't help laughing as well. Which meant we bumped into each other and that set us off harder.

"I am actually quite surprised to see you dance so well," I said.

He nodded. "Sometimes, in the security business, we double as escorts."

I stumbled and bumped into him without any laughter this time. "You mean you…?" I lowered my voice. "You mean you sleep with the clients?"

He blinked, totally unfazed. "I was referring to the whole escorting them to functions and the like. But…" He leant his lips to my ear. "There is a rumour swirling among the upper class that the Grace Grayson team guarantees complete…satisfaction…"

I burst into giggles and pulled back to look at him. "Seriously?"

Nico inclined his head in a way that was neither a confirmation nor a denial. "That's what I hear."

I looked into those blue eyes calculatingly. "Is there any truth to it as far as you could say?"

"Well I wouldn't be permitted to say. We're also prided on our confidentiality." He gave me a wink and I snorted.

"May I cut in?" The voice slid over my skin, sending tingles rushing over my body.

I knew I'd probably had a little bit too much to drink. It hadn't been enough to get messy, but it was enough to get giggly and chatty.

"Of course, boss," Nico said with another wink to me.

I bit my lip against a laugh and nodded to him, and Kit slid into position effortlessly.

"Hey," I said softly.

"Hi," he replied and the look in his eyes made my stomach flutter excitedly. "Having a good night?"

I nodded. "Yes. Thank you."

His eyes slid away from me for a moment. "You deserve it."

"I will pay you back for the dress one day." I waggled my head. "If I ever get a job that pays half as well as yours."

He chuckled and his grip on my tightened momentarily, as though he'd been about to tickle me or kiss me or something. Then he cleared his throat. "I'll make you a deal."

"Oh yeah?"

"Yeah. Get through your doctorate and we'll worry

164

about what you owe me then."

"What if I never finish it?"

His smirk was rueful and his eyes blazed with something that made tingles shoot through me. "Then I guess you're stuck with me."

Bare skin only touched in two places – our hands and my back – but it felt like everything ignited. It felt like nothing I'd ever felt before. I was no stranger to heavy petting, as it were, and Kit made me very interested just then in some *very* heavy petting. I kept replaying the almost-kiss from the night before in my mind and wondering what a real one would feel like.

Despite the champagne powering my system, I was determined to keep at least a semblance of cool.

12
Kit

I looked down and my heart thumped awkwardly in my chest at the look in her eyes. She was so light and free and happy that night and it hit me in a place I hadn't been aware I still had. And now she was looking up at me like there was definitely more.

I'd danced with a lot of women in my time, but none had felt like Amber. None had given me that feeling of butterflies in my chest and a goofy smile on my face I was barely able to hide. Certainly, none had had me cutting in out of jealousy. Something seemed to be zinging between us, something that I couldn't control and something I had no delusions was one-sided.

I wanted to pick her up and wrap her legs around my waist while we found the nearest surface and… And, while the look in her eyes suggested she'd be very willing if I kissed her, if I wasn't going to do something inadvisable then I needed a break. I gave her a warm smile and passed her off to her brother as soon as possible.

"She's something else, isn't she?" Rollie asked as I

dropped back into my seat.

I nodded. "She is."

Amber had danced with each of the guys and I'd watched her with each of them with no concerns at all. Except for the twinge of jealousy that hit me at the way she laughed with Nico. I couldn't get a read on the two of them, but she was comfortable with him and he with her. Which seemed odd on both sides. It was good. I wanted Amber to get along with the Grace Grayson team as much as I was sure Hawk did. I had far less reason to, so I wasn't quite sure why I did so much.

And I couldn't work it out while I was constantly distracted by the way her hips swayed in that dress. She was dancing with her brother, so there was nothing inherently sexual in the way she was moving. But I was fighting for control.

"Whiskey," I said to the waiter as he went by and Rollie held his hand for one as well.

Amber had spent all week messing up my tidy equilibrium and it was now totally shot. I needed to get my head on straight. I pulled my eyes off her and managed to get through most of the rest of the night without thinking of her in ways I really shouldn't.

We finally said our goodnights, being the last customers and realising we should really let McLean and his people pack up and go home. I invited the guys back but, as high as our tolerance for alcohol had become, if we were going to make it into work before midday, then we were going to need to sleep.

Amber gave each of the boys a hug goodbye, then I slid her coat on and we headed back to the Mayhew. She seemed to shiver a little so I put my arm around her as we walked and chatted about the evening.

She laughed. "Has Tank always been so–?"

Everything happened so quickly I barely registered it all. Amber was ripped out of my arm as she fell to the floor with a yell of surprise. I heard myself call her name as she said, "Johnson, I'm so sorry!" and I realised that she'd bumped into the doorman and they'd both fallen on the stairs.

"No, Miss. My fault. Are you okay?"

"Amber!" I called again and I held a hand out to her.

She smiled at me like she was waving my worry away. If only it was that easy. "I'm fine."

She took my hand but, as she put weight on her right leg, she winced.

"Oh, Miss. Are you hurt?" Johnson asked, concern marring his fatherly features.

Amber shook her head. "I'm sure it's just twisted. It'll be fine."

"I can get some ice?"

I steadied myself as Amber leant more weight on my arm. "Thank you, Johnson. I've got plenty upstairs. I'll see to her."

He nodded. "Of course, Mr Grayson. My apologies."

I gave him a short smile. "Accidents happen."

Johnson nodded and stepped back. I swung Amber into

my arms.

She squeaked, "What are you doing?" and put her arms around my neck.

"Carrying you up. Just a precaution."

Her eyes found mine for a moment and I realised how close our lips were. Her already flushed cheeks went redder and she bit her lip with a nod. She wanted it. I wanted it. But was it really such a good idea?

"Sure," she said softly.

"Good night, sir," Johnson said.

I nodded to him. "Good night, Johnson."

I carried Amber carefully to the elevator, not hating the feel of her in my arms.

"I'm sure I could walk," she huffed as she leant down to press the button.

"I'm sure you could," I replied as she put her arms around my neck again.

"It's not even that sore."

"Of course not." I felt the smile tugging at my lips as the door opened and Nigel looked up in shock.

"Everything all right, Mr Grayson?"

I nodded as I stepped into the elevator. "Amber just had a spill on the stairs."

"I'm sure I could walk by myself," she interjected.

"Just a precaution," I finished.

"Well, I'm sure Mr Grayson knows what he's doing, Miss Grace."

I felt her laugh. "I'm sure he'd like to think so."

"Hey!" I objected and she laughed out loud.

Nigel waved us into the penthouse since my card was a little difficult to get to and bid us goodnight. I carried Amber inside and put her on the bench.

"All right. Let me look at it," I said, trailing my fingers down her leg a little unnecessarily to slip her shoe off.

"Were you a medic in another life, Kit?" she teased and I looked up at her in humour.

"We've all had first aid training," I replied, taking her other shoe off and dropping it with the other on the floor.

She was looking at me with nothing but heat in those violet eyes and a playful smirk at those gorgeous lips. All thoughts of checking her ankle or getting her ice left my mind as I planted my hands on either side of her. She chuckled and I felt it in my cock.

It felt like we'd been waiting for one of us to move forward all night – fuck, for days. There were so many reasons why we shouldn't. I wasn't the relationship type, she was worth so much more than I had to offer, her brother would kill me if I touched her and he'd be none too pleased with her either. But I felt like I couldn't keep living on the edge like this without tasting her once. It took all my self-control not to kiss her.

She caught her lip in her teeth. "What would you say if I asked you to kiss me?" she asked teasingly.

"Ignoring the fact we shouldn't?" I asked, not even caring my voice was husky and desperate. I bent my nose to her neck and breathed in deeply.

"Why shouldn't we?" Her hand trailed up my arm tantalisingly.

There were so many reasons. I was just having trouble remembering what they were just then. "You know why."

"Because you're you and I'm me." Her voice came out with a slight sigh as her head tilted, giving me better access to her neck.

"And exactly who are we?"

Her hand rested lightly on my arm as I moved my nose gently along the skin of her neck and shoulder, barely touching her. "You're the arrogant, sexy guy who stars in the sordid dreams of anyone who sees you and I'm the twenty-three-year-old frumpy virgin geek."

"Have you seen yourself?" I asked her.

She took a shaky breath and I felt her lean into me. "I look beautiful *tonight*."

"You look beautiful every night."

Her breath caught for a second but, when she spoke, I heard the smile in her voice. "But you still can't kiss me?"

"That doesn't change the fact that my aggro best friend and your overprotective older brother are one and the same," I told her, my self-control waning steadily at the tone of her voice. She was demanding but coy, like she was playing at me being the one in charge when we really knew it was her.

Even so, she surprised me when her grip on my arm tightened and I looked into her eyes. "I still want you to kiss me."

I wanted to kiss her. I wanted to kiss her more than I remembered wanting anything in that moment. I shouldn't. I should stay strong, for Hawk if nothing else. But her knee hugged my hip tightly, pulling me towards her. She leant into me, her lips stopping close enough that our noses bumped and I could almost feel her.

"Kiss me, Kit?"

I couldn't take it anymore. Call me weak, call me stupid, call me insensitive. I'd own it all. But I needed to touch her. I took her cheek in my hand and pressed my lips to hers. Something bright and warm spread through my chest as her arms wound around my neck and she kissed me back deeply.

One taste of her and I was hooked.

I could taste the whiskey and chocolate on her as her knee hugged my hip. There was nothing else sweet about it and certainly nothing chaste. My tongue swept into her mouth, but she wasn't the submitting kind. And I didn't mind in the slightest.

"We really shouldn't be doing this," I panted between kisses.

"Probably not," she admitted, making no effort to pull away and, if anything, holding me tighter.

"Probably not," I agreed.

"We should stop," she said as she untucked my shirt.

"*Could* we, though?" I teased, hoping too late she'd understand my thoughtless words. It wasn't like me. She had me out of my mind.

"Probably not," she said against my lips. I felt her lips tilt in a smile against mine and knew she hadn't been offended.

"Do you want me to stop?" I asked her, knowing I didn't want to but would if it was what she wanted.

I felt her shake her head. "No." It was a forceful, definite answer and it was all I needed.

We were done with words and our kiss deepened. Her hand slid up my stomach under my shirt and mine slid up her skirt. As my thumb traced the inside of her thigh, she flinched and I froze. I started to pull away slowly but her hand shot out and wrapped around my wrist, keeping my hand in place.

"I'm sorry," I started. "I shouldn't have–"

But she shook her head. "I wasn't reacting to you." She looked up at me, those near-violet eyes boring into mine, beseeching something of me. "I want *you* to touch me, Kit."

"Are you sure? We can stop."

She shook her head again. "I want *you* to touch me, Kit," she repeated, pointedly.

She wanted me to understand what she was saying. And I did. My expression softened and I leant into her gently. "I'll go slow."

She nodded. As I moved forward to kiss her again, she pulled away slightly and said, "Just let me…" She frowned like she was confused or annoyed.

"Tell me what you want, what you need."

She pressed her lips together tightly before saying, "It

might sound stupid, but I just need to remember it's you."

I shook my head, brushing my nose lightly against hers purposefully. "It doesn't sound stupid at all." Slowly, I dragged my hands from her and placed them on the kitchen counter on either side of her legs.

"What are you–?"

"Shh," I breathed, leaning my lips to her ear. "Before I touch you, I want to tell you exactly what I plan to do to you…"

I felt and heard her suck a quick breath in and I was sure she leant towards me ever so slightly.

"I'm going to kiss you until you melt into me. I'm going to gently trace the soft skin of your inner thigh with my finger until I feel the heat between your legs. I'm going to kiss you until you feel nothing but me. I'm going to stroke you gently, bringing you to the brink of pleasure…" It wasn't until I felt her legs part further that I knew she really wanted it, that she was more mentally ready for it. So, I finished with, "And then, Amber, you're going to come for me."

I felt her jump a little and she pulled back to look at me. "What?"

My mouth twisted in a smirk. "You don't want to come for me?"

She opened her mouth, then snapped it shut. The look of total defiance that suddenly crossed her face was at odds with the heat of desire in her eyes. Finally, she cocked an eyebrow and said, "Willing and able are two very different things."

I leant into her and she watched me carefully, humour playing in her eyes. "By the time I'm finished with you, you'll be lost in such a haze of pleasure you'll have forgotten your own name."

"Those are mighty big words to say to a girl who's never had a single orgasm, Christopher."

I couldn't help but grin at her. "Oh, I plan to more than make up for that."

She laughed as she took my cheeks in her hands and pulled me to kiss her again.

"I've got you," I whispered as I ran my hand further up her thigh. "You're safe with me. But..." I stopped just shy of her pussy, noting the way she didn't even come close to flinching. She felt safe with me and that gave me that warm feeling in my chest.

"Kit?" She was disappointed and that made my cock twitch with pride and anticipation.

"We're not doing this here," I explained.

As I picked her up, she giggled and wrapped her legs tightly around my middle but she was looking at me questioningly.

"Bedroom."

I could see that excited her. "Yours or mine?"

"Mine?"

She nodded and I pressed another kiss to her lips before taking her to my room.

I put her down on the floor gently, helping her hold her

weight in case it hurt her ankle. She scrunched up her face adorably as she tested it, then she smiled.

"Tender, but okay."

"I'm glad," I said as I took her face in my hands and looked down at her.

I wanted her more than I'd ever wanted anything in my life. I wanted her more than I wanted to breathe. I wanted her more than I'd ever wanted to get Hawk home for her. It was dangerous but I had no inclination to shy away from that feeling. I recklessly leant into it in a way I'd never done before.

"Kiss me, Kit," she whispered, and those three words became my favourite.

So, I did. It was heat and passion and only all the good things in life.

Her hands pushed my jacket off my shoulders as I helped her out of hers. Our lips only parted when it was necessary and then found each other again quickly as we stripped each other down.

I could feel the hesitation in her now again, but there was resolve on her face so I spoke to her softly as I nuzzled under her jaw, reminding her it was me and I could feel her relax and hold me tighter again.

When we were both naked, I picked her up again and lay her on the bed, lying over her. She looked up at me with trust and heat and it made my breath catch.

I couldn't stop my smile as I trailed my fingers over her breasts, the soft skin of her stomach, and felt her shiver as I dragged them over her pussy. She drew in a sharp breath, but there was a smile on her face as her eyes closed and her back arched a little.

"You're with me, Amber," I murmured softly in her ear as I dragged my finger gently over her clit and watched in satisfaction as she bit her lip and let out a soft moan.

"Only one thing left on your to do list," she said with a smirk and I huffed a rough laugh. "You think you're up to it?" Her eyes opened and she looked at me steadily.

I nodded. "Yeah. I think so."

Her smirk grew. "We'll see."

I leant down to kiss her, and not just to shut her up. She threaded a hand through my hair as she kissed me back and I stroked through her wet folds lazily. I needed to get a feel for her, what she liked, what she didn't.

Her hips rocked almost sub-consciously to the rhythm of my fingers. As I rubbed over certain parts, she tensed and her whole body froze. But it wasn't that hesitation freeze, she was enjoying it. I knew I'd found the right spot when she pressed her forehead to mine and whimpered against me.

I increased my speed slightly, keeping my kisses leisurely. I felt her hand fist in my hair and her back arched off the bed. As she breathed heavily, I kissed her neck, her shoulders, her breasts, my fingers working her. She still had one hand in my hair and the other clenched the bedsheets under her as her body writhed to the rhythm we'd set together.

"You going to come for me, baby?" I whispered.

"Don't stop," she begged breathlessly.

13
Amber

Now this was definitely everything I'd ever played out in my fantasies. And then some. Kissing Kit was everything I'd dreamt of and more. But having his hand between my legs? That was even better than I'd ever imagined.

Before I'd totally given up trying, I'd felt that pleasurable build up a few times. That tight coil deep in your belly and the tingles in your clit. The way the pressure, the intensity grew, promising something wonderful at the end. It filled you full of excited anticipation and made you desperate for more. The way your muscles twitched like they wanted to get away and get closer all at the same time.

With Kit it was so much stronger than usual. All of it. My muscles did more than twitch, I was already shaking with the way he was making me feel.

And it wasn't just my sense of touch that was filled with him. His voice was in my ear, a slow steady calming reminder of him. Not that I needed it with my nose full of everything I'd ever associated with Christopher Grayson. That musky scent with a hint of sweetness and some sort of spice, as though he'd found his favourite aftershave at thirteen and never changed it. I'd had a small freak out before as unwanted memories had rushed in, but all that was gone now and I had trouble thinking of anything but Kit and the fact it was his hand between my legs. Finally.

His fingers slid down me and over my opening. I whimpered again, annoyed he'd broken the rhythm, but also enjoying his touch.

"Fuck. You're so wet," he practically purred as he teased me with his finger.

It slid ever so slightly into me then back out again before his fingers trailed back up to my clit and he began rubbing me again. It was the perfect combination of pace and force. Had I been doing it myself, this would have been the time I overthought it, my arm cramped up, and I ruined it. But I wasn't in charge. Kit was. So, I just lay back and let him work his magic.

"Don't stop," I panted again and I felt him shake his head slightly.

"I won't," he said as he took my nipple in his mouth as sucked on it gently.

And instead of all that twisting and knotting and coiling just fizzling out to an unsatisfactory nothing, it continued to build until I tensed around him, holding him tightly as my orgasm spread through me, tingling through my whole body.

I let go a breathy moan that was partly his name and shook harder with the force of it. As I rode it out, I stayed tense and chuckled in both nervousness and amazement.

"You right?" he asked, his voice tinged with laughter of his own.

I nodded, biting my lip as a shiver wracked my body again. "Yep."

Kit nuzzled into my neck, his hand sliding away from between my legs and up my side. My skin was far more sensitive than usual and I giggled as I pulled away from him slightly.

He looked up at me with a smile. "You sure?"

I rolled my eyes. "Yes. Did you want a medal?"

"For succeeding where even you failed? Yes, please." His grin was cocky and adorable.

I nudged him jokingly. "Too bad."

Kit's expression softened. "You sure you're okay?"

I nodded. "Of course. Why?"

He dropped his face and ran his nose along my jaw. "I just want to make sure you're comfortable. After…everything. I shouldn't have…"

"Shouldn't have what, Kit?" I asked, panic flooding me that he was regretting this already.

"I should have had better control," he said. His nose was still trailing over my skin gently like it was an excuse to not look at me. "I should have slowed down."

I leant my head against his. "I didn't want you to slow down, Kit."

And I didn't. Sure, some of it had been momentarily terrifying. But Kit had always oozed protection. Combine that with the few too many champagnes and the fact I'd been in heat for him since…forever, but especially the last week, and you got a pretty potent temporary distraction. All I felt now was amazing. But I wanted more.

I wanted new memories. I wanted to put my past behind me, where it belonged. I wanted to fully move on. I wanted to let go. I wanted to know once and for all that fear didn't rule me. And I had never felt safer with anyone outside my blood relatives than I had with Kit. At three, thirteen, or twenty-three, I felt safe with him.

"But I knew, Amber," he said softly. "I knew and I couldn't help it. You just…" He sighed heavily and pulled back enough to look into my eyes. "You test my limits. You make me forget…everything. It's embarrassing and amazing. But that's no excuse."

There was a warm fuzziness to the moment. Like we could say or do anything in this moment and it would be accepted, it would be believed. There was no hiding, just open communication and a swirl of emotions and sexual tension that felt as weird as it did right.

I took his cheeks in my hands and looked into his eyes. "I want this, Kit. I asked for this."

"But I–"

"If you'd said no when both of us wanted it, what does that tell me, Kit?" I asked him.

He blinked. "What?"

"What does that tell me?"

"I…I don't know."

"It tells me you think I can't make my own decisions. It tells me you think I don't know what's best for me. It tells me you think you get to make my decisions for me."

"Amber, that's not what I meant at all."

I shrugged. "Maybe not. But I can make my own decisions and it's my birth right to either live happily with or regret those decisions later, not yours. If you hadn't wanted to kiss me, fine. But don't go assuming you know what I want or what's best when I'm literally telling you what I want."

His eyes shone with the smile I was too close to see. "All right," he said finally. "I won't do that again."

"Good. Because there's something else I want, if you also want it."

"Oh, yeah?" he asked, nudging my nose with his. "And what's that."

"I want to have sex with you, Kit."

He paused and I wasn't sure if he liked or hated the totally outright way I'd said that.

When he finally spoke, he simply said, "I'd like that, too. But…"

"But what?" I asked when he didn't go on.

"But we're taking this slow and the moment you feel uncomfortable, you tell me to stop. No hesitation. No politeness. Just 'stop'. Okay?"

I could tell he wasn't going to do anything unless I agreed. And, all things considering – being the mad beating of my heart and my shortness of breath – I was happy to agree.

Nodding, I told him, "Okay."

He nudged my nose again with his, then kissed me softly. Everything about him was suddenly softer. It was – dare I even think it – romantic. I felt safe and loved and wanted in a way I never had before.

Our kiss was slow, our hands lazily tracing each other's bodies like we had all the time in the world, our bodies settling and moving together like they were made for it. His body was warm against mine and rougher in a ruggedly sexy way. His stubble rubbed against my skin – my cheek, my neck, my collarbone – as he trailed kisses all over me, but I liked it.

"You sure?" he whispered gently in my ear.

"If you ask me one–"

He planted a kiss on me and I could feel his smile. Then his nose nudged mine and he was looking into my eyes.

"Sorry. I can't help but want to protect you…"

My heart fluttered wildly and I took a deep breath. "And I appreciate it. But I know what I want."

A look passed through his eyes so quickly I wasn't sure I'd seen it right, but it looked like pain. "I'm still surprised that's me."

"You worried I'll change my mind?" I sassed, knowing now was no time for deep and meaningfuls. I wanted Kit to be my first and I wanted it to happen now, but I was worried we'd lose the moment.

I saw his smirk in his eyes. "Maybe."

"Then what are you waiting for, Christopher?"

He chuckled roughly, pressed another kiss to my lips, and reached over to the bed side table. He pulled out a condom and made short work of getting it on, then settled back between my legs.

"Just breathe, baby. I've got you," he whispered softly as he lifted my leg higher around his hip.

On my exhale, I relaxed and felt his tip at my entrance. A momentary flashback got me, but Kit's voice was murmuring steady nothings in my ear and I took a breath, filling my senses with everything that was him. I relaxed again and let my head fall back as he slowly started sliding into me.

I knew it would be worse if I tensed, so I spent so long trying to stay relaxed that I must have seemed really weird to him, because the next thing I knew he'd paused and was asking, "You okay?"

I looked at him and smiled. "Sorry. Trying to relax."

He sniffed against a smile. "Do you want me to stop?"

I shook my head against his pillows. "No. Sorry."

He kissed my neck as he murmured, "Don't be sorry. What can I do?"

I sighed as his lips trailed over me. "Nothing…"

"Nothing?"

"Mm…nothing. Don't stop," I breathed, then realised he'd slid the full way in and was thrusting slowly and steadily.

"You sure?" I heard the teasing in his tone.

My leg hugged him tighter. "I'm sure."

Still thrusting slowly, he drew back to look at me. "You're beautiful, Amber."

"You're not so bad yourself, Kit."

I took his face in my hands and brought him down to kiss me again.

It didn't take long for our bodies to fall into a perfectly-synced rhythm. I felt stretched, but it still felt good. All I could think about was him and me and us. I didn't worry about how right it felt, how it felt like I'd found something I'd been looking for my whole life but never realised I'd been missing. I didn't worry about the potential consequences of what we were doing. It was him and me and it was perfect.

Now and then, he'd murmur my name or, "Fuck," like he was feeling the same way.

After one such whisper, we caught each other's eyes and I was utterly stunned by what I saw in his. His smile was soft, sincere, and I felt all wrapped up in warm and fluttery tingles by the total lack of emotional walls between us.

Everything combined to give me this ditzy, little coy grin and his smile turned more cocky, it was more wry.

"You feeling good, baby?" he asked.

I nodded. "Yes."

"Good. You ready for a little more?"

I felt my eyes widen. "More?"

He was suddenly every part the gorgeous, sinfully sexy, arrogant guy, but I knew it was all for me. His half-smile was all cocky pride as his pace increased. My body arched towards him as my head fell back.

"Oh, shit," I breathed, my hand fisting the sheets under me as my other held him tighter.

"Good?" he asked, more like he was asking if I was okay than actually needing a performance report.

I nodded. "Good."

He brought my lips to meet his and kissed me hungrily as he pumped me harder.

That warming, tingling, coiling sensation started low and sluggish in me and I leant into him, wanting more of it. It was like Kit could read my every thought and movement. He held my hip firmly, making sure I kept my knee high.

"Fuck, Amber. I don't think I can–"

I shook my head against his. "Don't," I pleaded.

He kissed me again. It was hard and frantic and I gave him back as good as I got. Kit thrust into me faster and everything tingled in excited anticipation. The pressure in me built and I was sent over as Kit groaned in satisfaction, his forehead pressed to mine.

"Oh, shit," he breathed as he thrust slowly and lazily.

I huffed a laugh, which turned to proper giggles as he peppered me with kisses.

Then he was gone and dealing with the condom. I rolled over to watch his very fine backside, figuring I didn't have to pretend to not look at it this time. When he turned back to me, that sexy smirk was at full power.

"Like what you see?" he chuckled as he climbed back

into bed and snuggled us under his covers.

I nodded. "Very much. I always have."

"Oh, really?"

I nodded, stifling a yawn. "Really."

Kit gently brushed a piece of hair off my face. "You feeling okay?"

I smiled at him through sleepy eyes. "Perfect."

His smile was almost enough to keep me awake, but sleep was pulling at me pretty damned insistently. I saw his lips move, but didn't hear his words as I drifted into the best sleep I'd had in years.

14
Kit

I woke when my phone started buzzing on the nightstand next to me.

It took me a moment to work out what felt strange. As one hand flailed around for my phone, I opened a bleary eye and saw the reason with her damned beautiful hair splayed out all over my pillow and my arm. I was smiling before I'd fully registered everything that was going through my head.

I'd never woken up with a woman before that wasn't part of a job. I'd never wanted to. I'd also never had a woman in my bed since I was about eighteen. It made for an easier getaway when you were at theirs. Let them fall asleep, then slip out without any awkward discussion about repeat performances or number swapping. Some people called it cowardly, some called it a dick move, and I called it tactical.

But I'd watched Amber fall asleep the night before and felt nothing but warmth and happiness. I'd had no inclination to get her to her bed or to leave her there in mine. I'd wanted to hold her close and feel her heartbeat against mine as I let myself fall asleep. So, I'd done exactly that.

And now, watching her wrinkle her nose in her sleep, I had no inclination to leave her. But it was past nine and I needed to go to work. I needed to get to work and I was conflicted; I didn't want to disturb her but I didn't want to leave without saying goodbye either.

I managed to slide out of bed without waking her up – she just made my heart hitch in my chest at the way she snuggled down into my bed like she belonged there. I showered with a smile on my face and, when I was finished, she was still asleep. I carefully moved around my room as I got dressed, keeping my eye on the sleeping beauty in my bed. And I couldn't wipe the goofy smile off my face the whole damned time.

After I pulled on my jacket, I leant over and kissed her temple. "Have a good day, gorgeous," I whispered.

She didn't seem to wake properly, but she smiled and mumbled, "You too."

I had to stop myself skipping out the door like the grown arse man I was.

"Good morning, Donald," I said as I stepped into the lift.

"Morning, Mr Grayson. You're in a good mood for a Monday."

I smiled at him. "I am."

I don't want to admit it, but I'm pretty sure I had to stop myself dancing a little on the way to my SUV and I just had to hope the security cameras hadn't picked up my uncharacteristic behaviour.

As I drove to work, I wondered why the hell I felt so

good.

Yes, I'd been somewhat deprived of sex lately and it felt good to release all that pent-up energy. But it was more than that – I hadn't been this excited about sex since I'd lost my virginity.

It had to be Amber. It was something about that absolutely gorgeous little geek that had me smiling like an idiot. Something about that funny, sassy, beautiful woman that just made me crazy about her.

"Your best mate's little sister," I reminded myself and felt like I'd been dunked in another icy lake. "Fuck."

I punched the steering wheel as I pulled into my parking spot.

"Fuck!" I leant on the steering wheel and shook my head. "What the fuck have you done, you idiot?"

I took a deep breath and forced myself to relax.

"He's just going to have to deal. No. Better yet. He doesn't have to know," I muttered to myself as I got out of the car. "Talk to Amber tonight, then work out if Hawk does or doesn't need to know."

I had no idea what I was going to say to Amber, what our conversation would involve, but just at the thought of her I was grinning again.

"You are fucked," I told myself as I took the lift up to the office.

I was the first one in, unsurprisingly. But that was good because I caught myself humming along to the radio a couple of times. I didn't realise I was singing along with

'Original Prankster' until I heard a noise behind me.

I whirled, my hand instinctively going to my back, to find Rollie and Hawk standing at the door to my office and Rollie's phone camera was pointing in my direction. He was about to burst into laughter and Hawk was trying to shush him.

"What are you doing?" I asked, my eyes narrowing.

Hawk sniggered, "I haven't seen you even hum since basic training."

By the end of the sentence, he was full on laughing and Rollie had joined him. Both of them were in danger of folding in half from the force of their humour.

I pulled at my jacket and cleared my throat. "Guy's not allowed to sing now?" I muttered grumpily.

Hawk shook his head. "No. By all means."

"Camera's rolling," Rollie added eagerly.

I frowned as I stepped towards them and grabbed Rollie's phone. "Fuck off, the both of you."

Hawk smacked my arse. "And what's put you in this good mood?" he sang.

I shoved him away. "Nothing. I'm fine."

"If I didn't know any better, I'd say he got laid last night," Rollie chuckled as he helped himself to my chair.

I scoffed, feeling my mask fall into place. "I wish. I was too busy playing nursemaid."

Hawk nodded. "Ah. Bert put in some time worshipping the porcelain goddess, did she?"

I smirked. "No. She twisted her ankle on the way back

to the Mayhew."

Hawk lost a little humour. "She okay?"

She was okay enough for me to give her what she'd been lacking all these years. I cleared my throat again. "Yeah. Seemed fine. Little tender, but nothing broken."

Hawk nodded. "Good. Right. Well, unless you've got some more performing to do, what are the plans for the day?"

I shook my head at him and the three of us went over the day's agenda together until Tank rolled in around eleven looking a little worse for wear. Which was an interesting look on a guy his size.

"Bagel, mate?" Rollie asked and Tank visible gagged.

He shook his head. "Nope."

I smirked. "Get the man a bucket, would you Rollie?"

Tank glared at me. He disapproved of a lot really, but this disapproval took the cake for disapproving glares.

"Oi," Rollie said to him. "Don't blame us for being a lightweight."

Tank turned his glare on him and I knew it was mainly because he knew Rollie was right. Tank was the cheapest date among us. Unsurprisingly, Rollie was the most expensive – and that wasn't even taking into account his taste for the finest liquor.

I missed Tank's rumbled reply as Nico wandering out of the lift had caught my eye. He was wearing his tracksuit pants, his oldest Chucks, and his baggiest hoody. He still wore his sunglasses and his beanie was skewed to say the least.

"S'all right!" Hawk laughed. "Someone's pulled up worse than you."

Nico spared everyone the finger and disappeared into his office. He closed the door and kept the lights off.

"Next Champers Day. Less champagne…" Tank muttered, hauling himself off my couch and plodding to his own office.

"Has he got any classes today?" Rollie asked, spritely as ever as he bounced around despite having drunk Tank under about six tables.

I pulled up the calendar and sighed. "Yeah. Flo's coming in for one-on-one at two, then he's got a new client at four." I frowned as I went into the four o'clock one.

"What?" Rollie asked.

I shook my head. "VIP."

"Oh." That definitely had his attention. "I just so happen to be free at four o'clock. What a happy coincidence."

I looked at him to find him grinning winningly. If there was something Rollie did well, it was looking defiantly innocent and utterly cheeky at the same time.

"Don't get your panties in a knot, she's not like super VIP, she just has money to burn for discretion."

Rollie shrugged. "VIP is VIP. Can I? Can I, please!" He clasped his hands under his chin and batted his eyes.

I fought a smirk. "Fine. Yes. Last thing we need is Tank spewing all over her."

"I can do two," Hawk said, barely lifting his eyes from

his phone.

I shook my head. "Mrs Fortescue."

"Oh, fuck," Hawk muttered, dropping his phone into his lap, as Rollie barked a laugh. "What does she want now?"

"Escort to a lunch. Nothing big. Mr Fortescue apparently has other plans."

"What's he doing? I'll go keep an eye on him."

"Being married to her, probably shit he doesn't want a witness for, mate," Rollie laughed.

"Why me?" Hawk whined.

"She requested you," I said simply.

"Wait. What?"

I nodded. "She requested the presence of one Mr Patrick Grace for his – and I quote – 'cheeky elegance'."

Rollie snorted so hard he fell backwards, taking my chair with him. That should teach him to lean back on it precariously. Should. Wouldn't.

"Shit!" Rollie said through his laughter and that sent Hawk off, which sent me off.

Movement caught my eye and I saw Nico had stopped at my door, both hands wrapped around a mug and still wearing his sunglasses. Even then, I could tell he was scowling at us.

"How you holding up?" Hawk asked him.

"Fuck you all," was Nico's deadpan response. He took a defiant sip of coffee, gave us all a pointed disapproving look, and strode purposefully back into his office.

So of course, we all started laughing again.

"All right, what happened to our grumpy arse boss?" Hawk laughed.

I shrugged. "I have no idea what you mean."

"It's like invasion of the fucking body snatchers up in here," Rollie said as he dragged himself off the floor.

"You right?" I asked as he winced.

He huffed a laugh. "Oh, that's gonna leave a fucker of a bruise," he groaned as he finally got himself to standing. "No distractions. What's up with you this morning. We're all over here nursing hangovers from hell and your fucking giggling."

I sniffed against one of those full-blown goofy grins. "Nothing. I'm just in a good mood. So, sue me."

Rollie grinned as he hobbled towards the door, his hand on his hip like my grandma used to do. "Fine. Keep your secrets."

"You sure you're right?" Hawk called as Rollie kept on hobbling down the corridor.

Rollie's only answer was a flail of his arm in a general 'all good' motion.

"Right. Secret time," Hawk said to me when we were alone.

The guilt really hit me then. I'd never outright lied to my best friend before, but I was going to have to. "No secret. I'm just in a good mood."

Hawk leant towards me and scruitinised me intently. "I guess a week of Bert'll make a guy lose his mind after all." He smirked.

"Your sister's not that bad," I huffed.

"Nah, I'm joshing. I really appreciate you taking her in, man. I know how much she wouldn't have wanted to go home. And I know she's safe this way."

I swallowed, turning away from him so he couldn't see my face. "Nah. Of course. My pleasure." It sure had been.

"You don't know how much it means that you two are finally getting along."

I nodded. "I do, man. I do."

Hawk slapped my shoulder on his way out. "You both mean the world to me."

I let him go with no more than a nod. His tone told me that was the end of the conversation and I was okay with that. Hawk and I were never big on emotional declarations. When they were necessary, they were necessary. But neither of us liked being vulnerable, it reminded us of our mortality and impaired our ability to neutralise danger.

Besides, I didn't know if I could give him an answer that wouldn't betray the guilt I felt about his sister. Not that I was hampered by it for long and, on many levels, that made me feel more guilty. But I couldn't help it.

Rollie caught me actually literally spinning down the corridor at one point like I was about to break into a dance number. When I heard his snort, I even ran into the window of Hawk's office and it was obvious he'd seen as well.

So, that was how well my day went; I kept being caught out doing something goofy, the team would tease me, and I'd try not to do anything else stupid. Rinse and repeat. Too many times.

When I got home, I wasn't sure what I'd been expecting. But I was still in a brilliant mood. I felt like nothing could pull me down. And frankly, if my guilt and the team's teasing all day hadn't done it, then nothing was going to be able to.

Nothing except the look on Amber's face when she saw me walk out of the lift.

She was crossing the end of the hallway from the kitchen and looked like I'd just caught her stealing something. She was in jeans and an oversized jumper, her hair up and her glasses making her eyes bright.

"Hey," I said, dropping my bag by the door to my study.

"Hi." Her eyes darted around like she was looking for an escape route.

Something ugly hit me. If felt like Tank had punched me in the gut. I never wanted her to feel like that, especially not with me. The only reason I could think for her behaviour was something I fervently wished wasn't true; she regretted the night before.

"How was your day?" I asked, trying to keep my tone light and casual as I walked towards her.

She nodded and pressed her lips together. "Uh, good. Yours?"

I nodded as well, an uneasy trepidation filling me slowly. "Fine. I spent all day being teased mercilessly, but it was worth it."

Those violet eyes flew to me. "What? Why?"

I gave her a crooked smirk. "Apparently I'm capable of smiling."

Amber licked her lip, but it was a nervous action. "Oh. Well, that's good… I'm…" She cleared her throat as she looked at the floor. "Uh… I should–"

"Is everything okay?"

She looked at me like she thought I should know that, no, nothing was okay. Then she almost smiled as though everything was perfect. But then we were back to the wrinkled nose and biting lip of, no, nothing's okay.

Amber coughed as she pushed her glasses up her nose. "Look…about last night…"

She paused like she expected me to say it was a mistake, like she didn't want to be the one to say it. But I couldn't. I wouldn't. I didn't think it was a mistake. I felt guilty as fuck about what Hawk would think, but it wasn't a mistake.

"I'm not going to be the one to say it was a mistake, Amber," I said carefully.

"You don't think it was?" she asked.

I shook my head slowly. "No."

I couldn't tell if she elated or annoyed by that. Both emotions flickered over her face. "But Patrick?"

I nodded and swallowed. "Yeah." I raked a hand through my hair. "That… The situation's not ideal, but that doesn't make it…us a mistake."

I could see she wanted to believe me, but she was having trouble. And her eyes were imploring me to understand.

"I don't want to have to move out, Kit…" she said softly.

I had to swallow again against the sudden heat in my throat. "What are you saying?"

She sighed heavily. "I'm saying it can't happen again. I… It's not just Pat. Okay? I don't want to mess up what we've built this last week. I mean, we're friends now, aren't we?"

Now was decidedly not the time to tell her that I had no interest in being her friend. No, that wasn't right. If she was going to insist that was all we could be, then I was going to do my best not to fuck it up. But I wanted more. I wanted everything. I wanted to be her friend, her lover, her confidant. If she didn't want any of that though… Well, I'd live with it.

So, I nodded. "We are."

"Right. And…and maybe that's all we can ever be?"

Amber wanted me to say she was right. She wanted my permission that that's all we could be. I didn't want to risk driving her away, but I wasn't going to let her think the night before meant nothing to me.

"If that's what you want."

"You don't want?"

"I want us to be friends."

"Just friends?"

"Amber, I'm not going to lie to you but I want you to know I don't expect anything either…" I paused to make sure she understood what I was saying.

She frowned but nodded. "Okay. No. I want you to be honest."

"Last night wasn't a mistake for me. It never will be. Hawk can beat me black and blue, and I'd stand by our choice. But if you only want to be friends, then I accept that and that's all we'll be."

She pushed her glasses up again, then rung her hands in front of her. "I just…" She took a deep breath. "Pat means the world to me. You know how he'd react."

I did. I could handle it. We'd fall out for a while maybe, but I didn't want her to suffer for it. Hawk had been deadly serious in his threat to the team. He was fiercely protective of his little sister and he knew all us too well to think we'd be any good for her. But I wanted to be good enough for her and I was going to prove I could be, even if we were only friends.

"Yeah. He'd rip me a new one."

She nodded. "Exactly. And even if he didn't, what happens when…?"

She looked at me quickly, almost an apology, and I knew what she was thinking. She was thinking about what happened when her envisioned inevitable end of us occurred. If she wanted to be friends, telling her that I never wanted there to be an end was going to be incredibly unwelcome and, if I was honest, I wasn't sure I could promise her that just yet. My heart was convinced I'd want her forever, my head was a little more cynical.

"You know?" she continued and I nodded. "I just think it'd be smart if we put last night down not as a mistake, but just something we can't – shouldn't – do again. For everyone. I'd hate to lose you, Kit. And I know Patrick would never forgive me if we fell out again."

I could only nod. She was, unfortunately, right. Sex was all well and good – the sex had been phenomenal, to be honest. The driving, base need to protect her was great. But if I couldn't promise her anything then I had no right to possibly string us both along. We had too much history and too much potential future to do that to anyone involved. All of us deserved better.

"You're right."

Her relief was visible as she breathed out and relaxed. "Okay. Good. I was worried it would be weird."

I scoffed, putting on as much nonchalant bluster as I could muster. "Weird? No. It doesn't have to be weird."

"Exactly. I mean, we're both adults. Right?"

"Right."

"Capable of adult conversations and handling things like…adults."

"Definitely."

"Okay. So, we're agreed."

"We are. Friends."

"Friends." She gave me a small smile and pointed behind her. "I should really go and study, though…"

I nodded. "Sure. I'll organise some dinner a bit later."

"That'd be great. Thanks."

She gave me another smile, then turned and walked over to the dining table. I told myself my heart wasn't going with her.

15
Amber

Holy freaking Jesus. I'd had sex. With Kit. I'd actually finally lost my virginity and it was to my older brother's best friend.

I wasn't sure if I'd won the lottery or been cursed.

When I woke up on Monday, he was gone. I was naked and spread-eagled in his bed, and alone. I'd woken and felt amazing. I'd worn a goofy smile as I rolled around in his bed and breathed in deeply, just relishing his scent totally enveloping me.

By the time I'd dragged myself out of his bed, showered, dressed, and had a cup of coffee, that simple joy was fading and being replaced with doubt.

I couldn't remember him leaving. Had he not said goodbye? Why hadn't he woken me? Was he regretting it, so leaving was the easiest way to pretend it hadn't happened? What was going to happen now that it had happened? What was Patrick going to say if he found out?

I had no real answers. All I knew was that I was sure it shouldn't happen again. It was a one-time only sort of deal.

And he'd agreed. Right?

So, why did I feel like the only wrong choice we'd made was saying we'd only ever be just friends?

Every moment since he'd come home on the night before had been unbearable. The sexual tension alone felt enough to kill me. But trying to act normal been torture. Every time I thought I was definitely being normal, something minor would happen and I'd act even weirder in my effort to act normal.

Monday night after our talk had been okay. Kind of. Kit had actually cooked dinner for us, doing everything he could not to disturb me as he did. Even me and my amazing ability to dive into work and avoid my problems hadn't saved me from continually looking at him.

When it was ready, we ate together on the couch as we watched a movie. It was only awkward if I realised it was awkward. Or when we, for example, accidently bumped as I rearranged.

"Sorry," I huffed with a smile.

He shook his head. "All good." But I saw him swallow and wondered what else he'd been thinking.

I had to swallow myself or I would have asked him. And I was pretty sure that wasn't how friends were supposed to interact. Or was it? Now I was overthinking things again and all I could do was give him a stiff smile and shuffle closer to the other side of the couch.

After the movie finished, I actually counted to fifteen before I turned a smile on him and said, "I should probably get back to it. Geoffrey won't read himself for the sixth time."

Kit nodded. "Of course. I've got some work to check on anyway."

I also nodded. "Okay. Great."

And I went back to my work, all the while painfully aware of where in the penthouse Kit was without even having to see him. I could feel his hands on my body. I could taste his kiss. I could hear his voice in my ear, soft and low and the biggest turn on in human history. With all that going on in my head, poor Geoffrey didn't stand a chance.

So, I timed my exit perfectly to say good night to Kit but no more.

The next day, Tuesday, I gave the Cowardly Lion a run for his money and made sure I stayed in my room until I knew Kit had left. It was about as brave as I'd been in saying good night to him the night before, but I just didn't feel brave enough to face him when I couldn't get him out of my head.

Instead of trying to get him out, I chose distraction in a more guaranteed form. I put my music on as loud as I could handle, and started unpacking. It worked. Mostly. I had all my clothes put away – still barely taking up half the walk-in robe – and was feeling more stoic about the whole just friends decision as I made a start on the endless 'Bits & Bobs' boxes.

It was, after all, for the best.

The whole Patrick flipping his lid thing aside, I liked Kit.

We got along now. I didn't want that ruined when he realised I was boring and unglamorous. It was better we were friends, and I could still live with him and be in his life, without any risk that we were going to implode and ruin anyone's life.

It was a good plan. One I stuck to even better because he was working all night and I didn't see him. We exchanged a couple of quick messages because he'd wanted me to know what he was up to. But I didn't have to see him or smell him or have any other stark reminder of Sunday night.

Wednesday gave me a slight reprieve from my overactive brain in the form of Carmel and Flo, who stayed to have a coffee – or three – with me as her aunt pottered around the penthouse, taking her time with the cleaning and the tidying and going over the shopping list with me. Flo was amazing and I was a little bit in love with her by the time she left.

"So, Arthurian legend?" she asked me.

I'd exhausted the photos in her phone of her twin sons, Hank and Archie, and we were onto my PhD notes. It was like we trying to discover everything about each other in record time.

I nodded. "King Arthur and the knights and all that."

"Merlin?" she asked me excitedly.

I nodded. "And Merlin."

"Have you seen the show?"

I shook my head. "What show?"

She waved her hand at me. "Ugh. It's the best. The boys

are gorgeous. The bromance is real. I'll bring it for you next week when *Tía* comes."

I smiled. "Oh, I like that idea."

She pointed at me knowingly. "You can even call it research."

I laughed. "Yes!"

"Right?"

"And more Hank and Archie pictures, please," I begged.

She laughed. "That I can do. You don't babysit, do you?"

I gasped excitedly. "Cuddles? Ugh. I want to say yes, but I have *never* been left in charge of small humans before."

"I'll start you out slow," Flo promised and I smiled.

I decided without a doubt that I liked Flo from that moment on. I also decided that surrounding myself with new friends was probably a really healthy and sensible thing to do – I could only live in PhD world for so much of my life and I didn't really want no life awaiting me on the other end.

So, not only did I make sure to swap numbers with Flo – and promise myself that I'd actually charge my phone regularly – I also left the penthouse on Thursday. Yes, as in showered, dressed in society-approved clothes, and got into the Mayhew's elevator all by myself.

My mission? See if Petra wanted to go and get that drink.

With all the stuff with Dannie and Brent, I was most angry with Dannie. I wanted to say that I was surprised that she'd betrayed me like that. I mean, yes, I'd quite clearly not been terribly attached to Brent but that still didn't give a girl the right to sleep with her best friend's boyfriend, did it?

The more I thought about it, though, the more I realised I was resigned to her behaviour and the more I realised that she'd never been a terribly good friend to me through our whole lives anyway. She'd treated me like the DUFF – I was really only around to make her look better because I'd always been less outgoing, less concerned with boys, and less interested in behaving or dressing with the express purpose of getting a guy's attention.

And Farrah hadn't been much better. She'd always been more Dannie's friend than mine anyway, so I hadn't felt her absence at all. In fact, I'd actually enjoyed not having to put up with the drivel that came out of their mouths when they were together.

I just counted myself lucky that I'd been so angry with Dannie that I hadn't had time to miss her until I realised she'd always been a bit shit. As I walked into Petra's shop, there was a little bit of an ache in my heart where Dannie used to be. But I'd spent years in therapy learning to love myself again, so I knew when I was better off in the long run.

"If it isn't Amber Grace!" Petra trilled when she saw me.

She was measuring up an older women in a stunning gold dress I was willing to bet cost way more than even the one Kit had bought me.

I gave Petra a small wave and smiled at the woman.

"Just give me a sec to finish up and I'll be with you,"

Petra said, her tone all light and airy – much more so that it had been the week before.

Patrick had a similar tone. He called it his 'posh people' voice. It always made me smile when he used it, and Petra's was no different.

I sat in the chair Kit had occupied the other day and tried not to think too hard about him. Not like that anyway.

I tried to focus on the other things. The things like how he'd been with me during my panic attack. How he'd been with Dannie and Brent both times we'd seen them. How we'd actually been able to talk and laugh with each other this last week.

But no matter how hard I tried, I kept coming back to us in bed. It seemed inevitable and I couldn't stop it. It was like I was incapable of thinking about him one way without the other intruding.

So it was, as I waited for Petra, that I started to wonder if my pesky little awkward crush on Christopher Grayson had turned into something far more dangerous. I started to wonder whether maybe I was falling in actual, real love with my brother's best friend.

I wanted to say no. I wanted to say it was ridiculous. After all, everything I thought about him was strictly physical. He was hot. That was all. And my small teenaged brain, back when I naively hadn't really understood much in the way of reality, had liked swooning over his dark and dangerous vibe from a respectable distance. Right?

Wrong.

Apparently.

Because I might not have known much about actual, real love, but I had this annoying feeling that my feelings for Kit were becoming just that. That they at least had the potential to become just that. But I wasn't going to let them get that far. I was a strong, independent woman and I could totally make my heart not irrevocably fall for him.

"Something funny?" Petra asked and I looked up to see we were alone in the shop.

I also noticed I was wearing a smile that suggested I already knew I couldn't make my heart do jack shit. I sighed.

"Kind of. It's nothing."

"Fair enough." She dropped into the chair besides me. "What can I help you with? Fundraiser? Ball? Cocktail party at the Governor's house? Please don't tell me the team are taking you out again," she pleaded.

I pulled my head out of my heart and smiled at her. "Not that I know of, no."

"Thank fuck. I'm a jealous creature by nature and I'm just not sure I could be friends with you after that," she teased.

"On the topic of friends… That is actually why I'm here."

"Oh. I'm listening." She leant towards me.

"I was wondering if you wanted to get that drink?"

Her cheeky grin reached her eyes. "Um. Yes, please."

"I can repay you in a million Chaos and Hawk stories,"

I promised.

She waved my words away with a scoff. "Bah. I can take or leave those—"

"Really?" I asked.

"Pfft," she laughed. "Okay. Maybe not. But a drink sounds amazing though. I want to get to know little Grace." She took my arm in her hands and shook me gently in excitement.

I could understand that. I was also excited. "Excellent."

"When were you thinking?"

"I'm not fussy. When are you free?"

Petra thought about it for a moment. "How about tomorrow night? I can bring a change of clothes to work and we can be those classy bitches who hang out in the Mayhew's front bar on a Friday night?" She waggled her eyebrows at me encouragingly.

I nodded as I laughed. "Sounds great."

"Okay. Gimme your number so I can text you when I'm off."

We exchanged numbers and she hugged me before I left. There was an actual spring in my step as I strolled back towards the Mayhew. And, for once in my life, I actually enjoyed being out in a slight drizzle because I was in such a good mood.

My good mood lasted about fifteen minutes because Kit was home by the time I got back up to the penthouse. And it wasn't like the sight of him made me unhappy. It didn't. It made me happy. Just in less of an I'm-getting-my-life-together kind of way and more of a wow-look-at-the-way-he-looks-at-me, maybe-I-am-in-love-with-him kind of way.

When he saw me stepping off the elevator, he smiled warmly and I fooled myself for a second into thinking we were perfect as just friends. I fooled myself into thinking we could easily talk about each other's day or battle it out in *Street Fighter* without me ever wanting anything more than his friendship. But a second was all I needed to feel better about it. A second I could work on.

"Hey," he said as he loosened his tie.

"Hey."

"I'm surprised and impressed. You actually left the penthouse without coercion."

"I had an errand to run."

He was looking at his cuffs as he undid them, but spared me a sideways half-smirk. "I had half a mind to send out a search party."

I grinned. "A text might have been a little less drastic."

He nodded. "It might have."

"I was only down the road after all."

"Oh?" He was aiming for nonchalant, but I heard the almost-jealous question in his voice.

"Mm," I replied. "I had to see a girl about a drink."

I could see he was trying not to frown, and failing. "Dannie doesn't deserve—"

"No," I interrupted, practically giddy that he cared. "Not Dannie. If I see her in a million years, it'll be too soon."

"Good. You deserve better than her, Amber."

I tried not to flush at the sound of my name on his lips, especially when I was trying harder to forget the way it had sounded while he was inside me.

"Would you say Petra was better...?" I hedged.

He looked at me quickly. "You're hanging out with Petra?"

"It is, thus far, only a plan. Would it be a problem if I followed through?" Why was I sounding so weird? We were almost managing this normal thing and I had to go and be weird about it.

He nodded quickly and cleared his throat. "No. Of course not. It's not up to me who you hang out with."

It was a testament to my newfound feelings that I had a moment where I wanted it to be up to him; I wanted to impress him. I wanted him to think I made good decisions, decisions he agreed with. Then I remembered that was stupid and making decisions for a boy was stupid. Although how different really was it than making decisions we thought a friend or our family would think well of us for?

Not the point, I told myself sternly.

"So, it's okay I'm hanging out with her and it's okay if I happen to maybe leak a few secrets to her after a couple of drinks?" I pressed.

He smiled at me, but it didn't quite reach his eyes. "Petra's good people, Amber. And she knows exactly what the boys and I will do to her if she hurts you."

I smiled and tried for a joke. "Oh, I'm so uninterested in even thinking about a boyfriend right now." Which came out so well.

Kit coughed. "Ever?"

When any thought of 'boyfriend' currently had me believing no one could ever measure up to Kit and, even if we made a go of it, it couldn't last? Not really, no. Not that I was going to tell him the express details.

"Outlook not good," I told him.

He nodded. "Fair enough. Uh, what…? What plans did you and Petra make?"

"She said something about classy bitches at the Mayhew's front bar on a Friday."

Kit's smile was nostalgic. "Yeah. She would."

"What about you? Plans for tomorrow night?"

He looked at me uncertainly. "Uh. No. Not… Not at the moment. There has been some talk of trashing your high scores, though."

"Ah. Rollie, I presume?"

"Yep."

"Well, tell him to have at it."

Kit blinked. "No. Sure. I will. Permission kind of takes the fun out. But…"

"Yeah." I wasn't really sure what I was agreeing to.

Was this small talk? If so, I didn't care for it. We sounded so awkward. I felt like I was over-forcing the normality. Did I sound as stilted to him?

"Did you…have plans for dinner?" I asked him.

He nodded. "Work thing. Just have to change."

I clapped my hands in front of my body totally casually.

"Cool."

His parting look lingered and I know mine did a lot of lingering in return. I couldn't help it! Things swirled between us unspoken like I could feel them and I knew exactly what they were. And I wanted to answer them but, if I wanted Kit for the long-term, then just friends it was going to have to be.

I didn't want to speak ill of all those opposite-sex friends who made it work. I'm sure there were plenty of guys capable of being friends with his best mate's little sister. I'm sure there were other little sisters I could be friends with.

But me and Amber?

I wanted to do it. I wanted so badly to be what she needed me to be. But it was – figuratively and literally – hard.

Especially when she wandered out from her end of the penthouse on Friday night dressed in what could only be described as an outfit to eclipse all sexy librarian fantasies. She wore a tight-fitting sweater that accentuated all curves, a pleated plaid skirt that fell just above her knees, tights, and the sort of heels I remembered Petra calling booties. Her hair tumbled around her shoulders in soft waves and her glasses accentuated the make up around her eyes.

Hawk sniggered when he saw her.

"What?" she asked indignantly.

"I *was* worried about blokes eyeing you off all night."

So had I. I still was.

"What is that supposed to mean?" Amber asked and looked around at us.

Tank and Nico were looking at her as well, but Rollie took the distraction to finally KO Nico's fighter. He threw his arms up in the air, then looked around.

"Oh, hey," he said to Amber. "You look nice."

"Nice?" Hawk asked. "She looks like a grandma."

No. Nope. She didn't. And the situation in my pants was trying to be very vocal about that. I could be a gentleman and keep it to myself.

"She looks nice," Nico reprimanded.

"Nice?" Amber scoffed, looking down at herself. "I was kind of hoping for a little more than nice."

"I don't know why I spent so many sleepless hours worrying about you and the girls going out," Hawk said, matter-of-fact.

I couldn't help myself. I threw a cushion at him.

"What?" he exclaimed.

I pointed at Amber. "Your sister's hot, dude. Deal with your kinks on your own time."

"You think my sister's hot?" Hawk rounded on me. He was very close to the kind of face he used to pull back when we thought cooties were a legitimate threat.

I shrugged. "I have eyes, man. I don't need to apologise for that. And, if you were any decent kind of brother, you'd realise a lot of guys are going to be interested in that." My voice came out hard and disapproving in an effort to not give away how I really felt, and Amber heard every note crystal clear.

"So, is *that* supposed to change?" she sassed. "What's the consensus, boys? Is *that* frumpy enough to leave the house? Or should *that* go and change into something more appropriate?"

I frowned at her. "That's not what I meant."

"No. By all means, Kit. I'd *love* to hear your thoughts on the matter. If I recall, your particular preference is tall, legs for miles, bleach blonde, very little brains and clothes so tight they're really only a second skin!" she snapped.

None of us said anything – I think we were all too taken aback to come up with anything – and just watched as she struggled to get her coat on in her annoyance.

"Do you–" Hawk finally started but she huffed at him.

"I'm fine, thank you! I don't know why I'm even…" She dropped the coat on the back of the couch. "I'm only going downstairs."

She slid her phone into her pocket, then stomped off to the lift. When we heard the doors close behind her, we all let out a collective breath.

"I thought you guys were friends now?" Hawk accused.

I took a deep breath and forced myself to look at the TV. "Yeah. We are."

"Siblings fight, man," Rollie said encouragingly. "They're fine."

But were we fine? It didn't feel fine. Not when I wanted to kick them out and drag her to my room and give her a million reasons to never leave. And if I was honest, very few of them were sexual just then. It was unnerving, but I couldn't argue with the certainty I felt in my heart or my head.

I hadn't been able to promise her anything on Monday, but I'd had a week to think about whether the risk was worth the reward. I'd unanimously – yes, with one voter – decided that I was willing to risk anything for how I felt about her. I'd convinced myself that the way I felt about her was the kind of feeling you only got once in a lifetime. I loved Hawk like a brother, but there was nothing fraternal in how I felt about his sister.

The point was moot if she still only wanted to be friends. But at least I knew, if she ever changed her mind, how I felt about it.

Of course, if our most recent interaction was any indication of our future, then I'd spent all week wondering for no reason.

It still didn't stop me from keeping a not so subtle eye on the lift doors all night as I most certainly didn't wait for her to come back. Thankfully, Hawk was just as watchful so my stakeout wasn't indicative of anything that would get my arse kicked.

She rolled in at around one, obviously drunk but not messy. She kissed Hawk on the head on the way passed, said, "See, whole and still untouched," then said good night to us all and went to bed.

The team slowly dispersed over the next hour or so until I was left with an antsy feeling and a serious lack of wanting to go to bed. But I forced myself to not think about her and get some sleep. I was successful in so much as I managed to sleep relatively uninterrupted, but was thinking about her as soon as I opened my eyes.

"I need something stronger than coffee," I muttered as I dragged myself out of bed and to the kitchen.

I set the coffee machine on then went to my study to turn on my computer. Saturday morning was a shit time to be working when I wasn't expressly being paid, but if it took my mind off Amber then I was going to do it. I just needed to stop thinking about her long enough to get over her. That was a legitimate strategy, I was sure.

"Something about camping?" I wondered vaguely as I headed back to the kitchen.

"What?" Amber asked, just before I ran into her coming out of the kitchen.

I looked down at her, my hand going to her on autopilot to steady her. Her hand rested on my naked chest. Her eyes widened and I licked my lip. She bit hers and my heart rate spiked.

That sexual tension was crackling between us. It was like pretending this last week had only made it stronger. It was supposed to have put it behind us, we were supposed to have moved on. But every time I saw her smile at me, every time we inadvertently touched, I yearned for more. I told myself not to – she was my best friend's little sister, she was worth ten times better than I was, and we'd called just friends.

I watched her suck in a breath and bite her lip again like

she wanted to say something but something was holding her back. My skin tingled as it remembered the feel of her against it, of her fingers tracing the lines of my muscles and my ink. My heart constricted as it remembered the way she smiled at me, wrapped in my sheets and looking up at me with a shine in those beautiful violet eyes.

"Kit…" she breathed hesitantly. "I…I don't want you to think I'm ungrateful or anything…" Her chest rose and fell as she breathed hard. "But I can't do this anymore."

My stomach dropped. "You're… You want to move out?"

Her eyes widened in surprise. "What? No." She shook her head. "Us, Kit. I can't…I can't do—"

I cleared my throat and looked away from her. "No. I know. That's why we… That's why we're keeping our hands to ourselves. Just friends." I took a step back, but she took my hand and I looked back at her.

"No. That's what I'm talking about, Kit. Keeping our hands to ourselves. I can't… I don't want to…"

I had never felt such hope as what I hoped she was saying. "What…? What do you mean, Amber?"

"I don't want just friends, Kit. I want you."

I searched her eyes. "You want me?"

As she squeezed my hand gently, she gave a breathy chuckle that had me fighting for control. "I've wanted you for years."

I felt my eyebrow quirk and the corner of my mouth go with it. "Really?"

She nodded and her cheeks flushed slightly as she looked at my chest. "It's not a new thing. Honestly, I've…" There was that confidence I loved. "I've always been awkward around you because I've always had a thing for you. The thing's changed a little over the years, obviously. I wasn't desperate for you to throw me on your bed at thirteen or anything. But…"

I took her cheek in my hand and she stopped talking as she looked up at me again.

I'd felt it on Sunday as she'd been so confident that it was me she wanted. And I felt it again. Why me? How me? I didn't want to question my luck, but I couldn't help it.

"You didn't hate me?" I asked.

"Hate you?" she spluttered, smiling. "No. I… I thought you had a terrible lack of morals through most of your teen years. But I never hated you, Kit. I was just a little embarrassed I was crushing on someone who'd never look at me twice."

I felt like all my wildest dreams were coming true. I didn't have to wait for the day I found out she really did hate me, because she never had. Not only did she not hate me, she wanted me as much as I wanted her. And the idea I'd never look at her twice?

"That's not true," I said softly. "I mean… It probably *was* true then, because you were fifteen last time I really saw you. But it's not true now. Everything I want to do to you now is totally legal."

Her eyes shone and she caught her bottom lip in her

teeth. It wasn't hesitance this time, it was desire. I watched her take a deep breath as a smile crept across her face. "What exactly do you want to do to me, Kit?"

Fuck. I shouldn't have started this.

No. I wasn't the only one who'd started it. She'd made the first move. Again. She wanted me as much as I wanted her – the *way* I wanted her – and I wasn't going to keep making excuses to myself anymore. She was gorgeous, she was funny, she was tantalising, she was sweet. Hawk was going to be epically pissed but, we'd already crossed the line once, he could hardly get angrier.

I looked down at our joined hands and while I could picture every little thing I wanted to do to her, every touch I wanted to give her, every caress I wanted to draw out, every time I wanted to hear that breathy moan in my ear, again and again. But my lips wouldn't make the words and there was only thing they wanted just then.

"To start with, this…" I said softly as I leant down and pressed my lips to hers.

Our fingers intertwined and she stepped closer. My heart hitched and, for one brief moment, everything felt perfect. For one moment, I honestly believed I could have that other life. And this time I wanted to stay with that feeling, with her, for as long as I could.

Her hand slid up my chest and I felt goose bumps break out across my skin. My arm wrapped around her waist, bringing her closer to me. As she rose up on her toes, she cupped my cheek. She leant her forehead against mine and let go a breathy laugh. Her eyes were still closed.

"To start?" she asked with a hint of cheek.

This was the Amber I wanted, the one with the confidence who always called Hawk out on his crap, the one who didn't put up with my crap. Only now, she could look me in the eye while she wasn't putting up with my crap. I wasn't about to dismiss her demons, but it seemed they didn't have quite such a hold on her anymore. And I wanted to do whatever it took to keep it that way.

I picked her up and put her on the kitchen bench, trailing kisses along her cheeks, her neck, her jaw. "To start. To finish. And everything in between."

Her smile made her eyes shine with not just fire but life. "That's an awful lot, Christopher," she said.

I drew back only far enough to look at her, planting my hands to either side of her. "I couldn't promise you anything before, Amber. And I don't know how much you want me to promise you now. But I want to make a proper go of this. I don't want to miss out on what could be the best thing in my life because I was too afraid of the future."

"I thought Pat was the best thing in your life?" she teased.

"Maybe it's my destiny to love all Graces," I replied as I searched her eyes.

"You love me?"

I smiled at her. "I don't know yet, but I'd like to find out."

She wrapped her arms around my neck and her leg

around my hip, using them to pull me closer to her. "So would I, but what about my brother?"

"I don't know about that either."

"Hm. I get that."

Thank fuck. "You do?"

She nodded slowly. "I don't really want to be the one to tell him you scored his little sister's virginity, do you?"

I wrinkled my nose in thought. "Especially not when you put it that way."

"So, I'm proposing–"

"Already?" I teased and she grinned widely.

"Funny. No. I propose we wait a bit."

"Wait?"

"Yes." She nodded. "He's not going to be the only one with questions."

"So, maybe we wait until we have answers to those questions?" I finished and she nodded.

"Not long, just…?"

"Give it a week?" I suggested.

"A week. Sounds good."

"A lot can happen in a week," I told her as I wound my arms around her.

"Is that so?" she laughed.

I nodded. "It is."

"Like what?"

"How many orgasms do you think I could give you in that time?" I asked.

Her laugh was pure and happy and lit me up inside. "Um.

I couldn't even begin to guess. I don't know that you *have* to give me any."

I shrugged. "Well, of course. I don't *have* to do anything. But I'd quite like to make up for lost time."

"Lost time?"

"Yep."

She bit her lip like she wasn't sure about voicing her next thought.

"Tell me everything," I begged.

"What if I just want to feel you?" she asked, a slight flush creeping up her cheeks.

I nuzzled into her. "You want to feel me?"

She nodded as her arms tightened around me. "I want to feel you. Right here is fine."

I felt a smirk break unbidden. "You asking me to fuck you on the kitchen bench, darlin'?"

She laughed as she pressed her face to my shoulder. "Sure. I'm asking you to fuck me on the kitchen bench, Christopher."

I leant back and made her look at me. My eyebrow quirked and I couldn't have wiped the half-smirk off my face if I'd wanted. "You want it? Because I'm more than happy to oblige."

She drew me back to her, one hand trailing down my chest. Every nerve came alive and fucking sang for her. Her lips brushed against mine as she said, "I want it."

"Fuck," I moaned. "Your wish is my command."

She kissed me hard and her hands dropped to my waist

band. I took hold of her wrists.

"Uh-uh," I said against her lips. "You were in charge last time. My turn."

Exaggeratedly slowly, she raised her hands above her head, a cheeky humour in her eyes. "Have at it."

This woman was going to be the fucking death of me. And I was going to enjoy every single second I had with her first.

I kissed her hungrily. I kissed her like I was never going to get enough of her. And she gave back as good as she got. She wasn't shy. She wasn't submissive. She knew what she wanted and it was hot.

My hand skimmed up her leg and I realised she was only wearing that oversized jumper. My fingers trailed up further to her hip and I discovered that was really all she was wearing. I felt myself smile against her as I slowly dragged her jumper out from under her arse.

"Not an accident, then?"

"You complaining?"

I shook my head. "Fuck, no."

I brought her closer to the edge of the bench and pressed against her. Her eyes closed and she licked her lip before wrapping her body around mine and kissing me

"Wait. Wait. Wait," I muttered, sliding out of her grasp.

"What?" she asked, confusion and hurt marring her features.

"Condom," I told her, pressed a kiss to her lips, then ran to my room.

When I got back, I didn't go back around into the kitchen. I reached for Amber's arm and pulled her across the bench to me. She yelped and laughed as I wrapped her body around me again with one arm while I ripped the condom open with my teeth.

"Keen?" she teased.

I nodded. "Embarrassingly keen." I grinned.

I pulled my cock out of my shorts and gave it a few swift strokes as I looked at her. She was so fucking beautiful. Outside, yes. But what made her beautiful on the inside just made her all the more gorgeous to my eyes.

"You sure—"

"Kit!" she huffed.

"I was only asking about the kitchen, baby."

She wrapped herself tighter around me. "To start with."

My eyebrow rose. "To start?"

"I want to try everything."

"I'll do my best to accommodate."

I rolled the condom on, then took hold of her hip and brought her to the edge of the bench again. Pressing into her, I rubbed my cock through her folds. She moaned softly and her arms tensed around me.

As I kissed her, I ran my fingers between her legs. She was wet and ready. I guided myself into her gently, kissing her deeply. She relaxed around my cock just as she held me tighter.

I started thrusting, again astounded at how she made me feel. Nothing had ever felt more right, more perfect, than our bodies moving together. Her fingers threaded through my hair as I held her hips firmly, her legs wrapped around my waist. My thrusts came harder, faster, deeper, and she moaned against my lips, pulling me even closer.

One hand ran up her back under her jumper. She pulled away only long enough to help me get it off her then our lips met again in frenzied passion. She nipped my lip gently before pressing her forehead to mine and looking into my eyes. There was total abandon in there, pure wanton desire and a hefty bold streak that called to something in me.

"Harder, Kit," she panted.

"Harder?"

She nodded. "Harder."

She wanted it? I was happy to give it. So, I did. I put my hand on the back of her head and kissed her as I pumped into her faster, harder. Her hand gripped my back, her nails digging into my skin, and her head dropped back, so my lips trailed to her neck.

"Oh, God! Don't stop, Kit. Don't stop!" she moaned and you can bet I wasn't planning on it.

She was warm, she was tight, and she was very close to breaking every ounce of control I'd ever prided myself on. I was too close. I slid my hand between us and found her clit. She whimpered. It was so sweet and so sexy, it amped up the tightness in me, but I hoped it was going to be enough for her.

It almost wasn't. I finished first, but didn't let up until I felt her tighten around my cock and her body contract around mine. She cried out in pleasure and was shaking around me as I gently slid my hand out from between us.

I took Amber's face in my hands and kissed her softly as I slowly slid out of her. Her hands rested on my chest as she kissed me back. Everything about her was languid and soft. Until she looked at me and I saw that had done nothing to sate the desire in her eyes.

"What's next?" the little minx asked and all I could do was laugh breathlessly.

17
Amber

"Shit. Shit. Shit," I muttered as I finally caught sight of why my phone had been vibrating like mad for the last half an hour

I scrambled out of Kit's bed hurriedly. Kit's bed. The bed I'd been in all night. Again. I was sore, but a good kind of sore. Which wasn't surprising considering that Kit had had me in the kitchen, on the lounge, and twice in bed before we finally fell asleep – or passed out in complete sated exhaustion in my case.

"What's the matter?" he asked.

I turned to look at him and tried very hard to ignore the very obvious desire in his eyes as they roved over me unashamedly. It made me want to get back into bed with him. So badly. But I couldn't. I sighed.

"What?" he asked.

"Don't you with the sexy morning voice, Kit," I chastised and he chuckled roughly.

I leant my head back for a moment as I prayed for the strength to walk away, then grabbed one of his shirts from where it was lying on the bedroom floor and pulled it on.

"What's the rush?" he asked me, and I knew he had the same thing on his mind as I did.

"I've got six missed calls from Mum!" I hissed. And I didn't want to call her back while I was in bed with him because that would be…weird.

But just as I turned to get my glasses, he grabbed my hand and drew me to him.

I was damned powerless. He was addictive and made me feel things I'd never felt before. Things I wanted to keep feeling. Things I was finally going to let myself believe I deserved.

Not even pretending to put up a fight, I let him pull me back onto his lap. Kit ran his hands over my hair and down my back as he looked me over like he was committing me to memory. There was a softness in his eyes and his smile, like he was actually happy. I couldn't remember the last time I'd seen him look like that, but it made a burst of warm giggly delight burst in my chest.

His hands went to my hips as he pressed a gentle kiss to my lips. It wasn't fevered. It wasn't maddening. It didn't leave my clit tingling for more. It was different. It was precious. It was sweet. And the only thing tingling was my heart as his nose nudged mine.

"I have to ask…" he murmured against my lips.

I wrapped my arms tighter around his shoulders. "What?"

"What made you change your mind?"

"A lot of things."

And they had.

For starters, I hadn't been able to stop thinking about the very real possibility I might have gone and fallen in real, actual love with him. There was also his audacity in his disapproving of my outfit the night before that had made me think just friends wasn't going to work quite as well as we'd hoped. There was the fact that I was horny as hell for him. And, there had been a tonne of alcohol and a vague discussion with Petra in which we both decided you only live once – it was good to have a friend again.

"What sorts of things?" he pressed.

I smiled softly, deciding that it was worth putting it all out there. I'd either already set things on to a course to implode everyone's lives, or it was going to be amazing. There wasn't any in between anymore.

"Mainly this feeling that, whatever this is…it's special. I don't quite know what it is, but it's not just sex. I mean, I'd like to have a lot of sex with you, but I don't want it to *just* be sex."

He chuckled. "I'm glad you feel that way."

"You do?"

He nodded. "Yes. Because I feel the same way." He ran a hand over my hair again as he looked me over once more. "I can't put my finger on what it is. It's just you. I want to be better for you. I want to be better with you–"

"You're perfect the way you are, Kit."

His smirk was rueful and it was sexy. "I think you might

be biased."

I shook my head. "I know you, Christopher Barrett Grayson. I know who you are under all that sexy muscle and ink and brooding seriousness. I always have."

"And who am I?" he asked.

I opened my mouth, but my phone started buzzing next to my leg. I looked at it and saw it was Mum ringing again.

"She's just going to keep calling," I sighed.

He kissed my neck. "So, answer it."

"I'm on top of you," I pointed out.

"I'll be quiet as a mouse," he promised and I smirked.

"Hello?" I answered.

"Why am I just hearing about Brent now?" Mum asked and I grimaced.

Kit looked at me in question and I shook my head as I clambered off him. He didn't stop me this time.

"What do you mean?" I asked, trying to act innocent for all the reasons.

"Patrick just made it painfully obvious that he was letting something slip. Why didn't you tell me? What happened? When?"

I sighed as I pulled on my sleeve. "Exactly what did Pat tell you?"

"Just that you and Brent were over. I mentioned Christmas this year and he said Brent wouldn't be coming."

I wrinkled my nose at Kit in frustration and he looked at me with a mixture of confusion and humour.

"Ah… Okay. Look, Mum. I… I walked in on Brent and

Dannie, and I… I left."

"You… You left? They were…?" A pause. "Oh, baby. How are you?"

I knew what she was really asking. "I shoved it down, it bit me in the arse and I…" I looked at Kit and gave him a smile, knowing I'd never have to hide any of that from him. "I dealt with it. So, I'm okay. Still a little pissed off, but I'm okay."

"Are you sure? Where are you? Patrick didn't say you were staying with him."

"Uh, no. I'm… I… We actually ran into… Into Kit and he… Well, I've moved into one of his spare rooms for now."

Mum actually squealed in excitement and I nearly dropped my phone. "Oh my God! Yes! Family dinner!"

I blinked. "I beg your pardon?'

"Yes. If you're living together, you have no excuse to not be in the same room together anymore and we can have a full and proper family dinner."

Of course, that was the first thing she thought of.

"Uh…" I started.

"Is he home?"

Uh, yeah and sinfully gorgeous first thing in the morning. "I think so."

"Go and ask him."

"About what?" I squeaked.

Kit's head tilted in question, but I could see his lips had other ideas.

"Dinner," Mum said like it was obvious.

"Sure. When?"

"Tonight. Phil and Angela are coming anyway. I'm sure they'd love to see Kit. I'll call Pat and text Ange to call Angus."

"Uh… Wait, he's just walked in. I'll ask him."

"Ask me what?" Kit asked, a cheeky smirk at his lips.

"Dinner tonight with the folks?" I opened my eyes wide, wondering why that didn't elicit more panic out of him.

He nodded. "Sure. That'd be great, Mags," he called loudly enough for her to hear.

"Oh, wonderful!" Mum said.

I frowned at him. "What time do you want us?" I asked Mum.

"How's six-thirty?"

I nodded. "We'll be there."

"You'll pick Pat up?"

"Sure."

"Wonderful. Thanks, Bert. Love you!"

"Love you, too," I said, but she'd hung up. "This is going to be interesting."

Kit coaxed me back into bed. "I can think of something more interesting…" he said, his voice low and sexy.

"Oh?" I asked. "And what's that?"

"You and me in bed. At least for another few hours."

"Hours?" I clarified.

He nodded, a heat in his eyes that I felt shoot right through me. "Hours."

"I could be persuaded," I said.

His lips dipped to my neck. "Preference of method?"

I laughed. "Surprise me."

With one strong arm around me, he reached behind him and grabbed a condom out of his drawer. "How's this for a start?" he asked, his smile bright in his eyes.

"That all depends on what you plan to do with it."

Kit leant forward and nipped my earlobe gently before whispering, "I was planning to put it on my very hard cock and gently slide you onto me."

"And then what?" I teased, very much liking the sound of that.

I felt his smile just under my jaw. "Well, I was thinking we could just sit here and talk about your thesis progress."

I laughed as he hugged me tightly and I hugged him back. "You just know the direct path to a girl's heart, don't you?"

"You don't think so?" he asked as he trailed his nose across my cheek.

"I think I like the first part of your plan—"

"But not the second?"

I shook my head.

"Who made you in charge?"

"Oh, I think it's my turn, isn't it?"

He grinned at me cheekily as he held the condom to me in two fingers. "Why, yes, it is."

I took it and rolled it over him. He breathed out slowly as though I actually managed to test his control and I loved every minute of it. My hand stroked him slowly a couple of times, our eyes on each other a challenge.

"All right," he said with a wry half-smile. "I yield."

He helped me out of his shirt as I knelt up to position myself over him.

****

As soon as the car pulled up in the driveway, Patrick was out the door laughing about how funny it was going to be to have all of us in a room together for the first time in almost a decade.

"So, we just act normal and no one will know," I said, looking at Kit.

"We don't act normal together anymore, Amber."

I shot him a glare. "If Pat finds out before–"

Kit took my hand. "That's not what I meant," he said softly, looking up at me. "We get along now, Amber. We can talk to each other. The other stuff is great." He gave me a sexy half-smile. "Better than great. And we can hide that stuff. But Hawk's not the only one who's going to notice you can look at me now."

I nodded. "No. Sure."

Patrick knocked on the door. "You coming, or you both ditching me here?"

I pushed the door open into him with a saccharine smile. "Keep your pants on," I told him.

"My pants are fine, thank you," he retorted as the three

237

of us headed to the front door.

Mum had it open before we got there and there were actually tears in her eyes. "Oh my God. It's a dream come true. Dream. Come. True. Angela!" she yelled into the house. "Look at you. Angela! All three of you together again."

Angela appeared at the door and she was just as excited. "Oh, look at them!"

"Mum," Kit said tightly. He'd always silently suffered his mum's affection.

Both mums rushed forward and hugged their boys. I snuck inside and hoped I could avoid the overzealous welcoming committee.

"Amber!"

I turned and there was little Chaos 2.0. Angus Grayson. Nicknamed Toad by Kit and Pat when he was about two. At twenty-four, he was the near spitting image of his older brother, just a little bit less in every way. But he was still one of my favourite people and much more like a brother than Kit would ever be.

"Angus!" I went over to hug him.

"You're looking good, considering."

I rolled my eyes and shoved him playfully. "Thanks. Parentals catch you up?"

He nodded. "Why didn't you tell me?"

"I thought you were still in Japan."

"You were in Japan?" Kit asked from behind me and I felt his hand brush my back.

Angus looked up at his brother and years' worth of history flooded me. The two brothers had never really got along. They loved each other. They respected each other. Kit was Angus' hero – not that he'd ever admit it out loud. But they weren't friends.

"Yeah. Holiday with the boys," Angus replied.

"Cool. Have fun?"

Angus lost most of his awkwardness – reverting back to the younger sibling desperate for his older brother's approval. I knew the feeling well.

"Yeah. It was great."

"Well, well," came Phil Grayson's voice. "If it isn't a full house."

"First time in how long?" Dad asked.

"About ten years, I reckon," Phil said.

"At least," Angela said.

"It wasn't the boys' eighteenths was it?" Mum asked.

"You know, it might have."

"No, it was Christmas," Phil said.

"Oh!" Mum cried, laughing. "Yes. It was…"

I quickly sidestepped it out of there and into the kitchen to find some booze to get me through the night. As I pulled myself out of the fridge with a beer, I saw Mum next to me.

"You're looking good, baby," Mum said, bumping her hip into mine.

I nodded. "I feel good."

"I worried. When we talked earlier, I worried. But you're really looking good."

I looked at her. "I told you I was good."

"And does this have anything to do with Kit?"

"Mum!" I laughed, but my heart pounded. "Ew. No."

Mum snorted. "Oh God, no! I didn't mean like...No!" she giggled.

I huffed an awkward laugh. "No. Good. Me either. Because ew."

"What's ew?" Pat asked as he came in.

"Kit and Amber," Mum giggled.

I heard a spluttered cough and turned to see Kit was behind Patrick's grimace of disgust.

"That's not ew," Pat said. "That's illegal."

I swallowed hard and caught Kit's eye.

"Oh," Mum tsked with a laugh. "It's not illegal. It would be weird though. Ange and I always wondered if Amber and Angus would get together. Didn't we, Ange?" Mum called into the other room.

"Ew." I wrinkled my nose.

"Toad?" Kit asked as though it was laughable.

"Yeah," Patrick added. "He's not nearly geeky enough."

Now I was spluttering a cough.

"You right, Bert?" Pat asked as he got a beer out.

I nodded. "Totally fine."

Mum ushered us out of the kitchen and the Grace Grayson clans spent the evening catching up on everything. There was a lot of pooh-poohing Dannie and Brent which I thought was sweet, but the way Mum and Angela cooed over how sorry they were my relationship was over in front

240

of Kit made me feel weirded out.

When I ran into him in the bathroom before dinner, all I could do was hug him.

"I'm sorry," was the first thing out of my mouth.

"For what?" he asked.

"For our mums and all the Brent stuff."

He looked at me like he wasn't sure if it was funny or my reaction was sweet. "It's fine, darlin'."

"Because it doesn't bother you... Because we're–?"

He took my hand. "Because it's in the past and there's nothing I can do about it."

Kit had always been annoyingly good at looking like nothing bothered him and I'd always had trouble seeing through him. I couldn't tell now if he was legitimately not bothered, or just hiding it really well.

"It's fine," he said gently as he leant down to me.

I looked behind him as I put a hand on his chest. "Kit!"

"What?"

"No one knows about us. What are they going to say if the see us kiss?"

"We should tell them."

Panic surged as I tried to reconcile telling Patrick with his reaction to our hypothetical relationship. I couldn't do it. Not yet.

"I just... I need some more time."

"If you've changed your mind...?"

I shook my head wildly. "No! No. I want this. I want you. Us. I just...need a bit more time before I piss my brother off."

He nodded slowly. "Okay. But my silence can only be bought with a kiss."

I smiled. "Kit!"

"What? One kiss? A little kiss? Please."

I leant up and kissed him quickly. "Happy?"

His hand went to my cheek as he kissed me again. "Happy."

"Okay. That has to be it." I kissed him one more time. "Someone will see."

"No one will see," he said, drawing me back to him with a mischievously tempting smile on his face.

Just as I was about to kiss him again, we heard Patrick getting closer. "…don't know. Is it in the linen press?"

Kit and I stepped away from each other just as Patrick opened the door. He looked between us and blinked.

"Uh, hey," he said slowly.

"There's a line," Kit said and I nodded as I stepped towards the toilet as though I was going in there.

Patrick grinned. "Go use the en suite," he said to Kit as he pulled open the linen press "Waiting around like a chump. Bert, you know where Mum's quote 'good napkins' are?"

"I'm gonna…" Kit started.

I nodded. "Good. Yeah. Okay." I tucked my hair behind my ear and went to help Patrick.

"I thought you were peeing?" he asked as Kit sidled out.

I huffed. "You know I don't like an audience."

Patrick just laughed and nudged me as we continued the hunt for Mum's good napkins.

I knew Kit was right. We had to tell everyone. I'd asked for a week. A week to work out what the hell I was going to say to my big brother. It wasn't lost on me that we were sneaking around behind his back in a very similar manner to the way Dannie and Brent snuck around behind mine. I didn't want Pat to find out by accident, I wanted him to hear it from us because we – and I mean I there – manned up and told him.

The prospect was just terrifying.

18
Kit

It hadn't been a week. It had been two weeks. I'd been hiding my relationship with his little sister from my best friend for two weeks. And the fact that the 'R' word didn't make me recoil in disgust even in the privacy of my own brain told me that I really needed to tell him. I just wasn't sure if any of us were ready.

"I'm in love with Amber."

I looked around like maybe it hadn't been me who'd just blurted that fact out in front of my whole team at our daily staff meeting.

"Well," Rollie said. "Hands up who expected that."

Tank was looking between Hawk and me like he was concerned about the state the carpets were about to be in. Nico raised his hand without looking up from his computer and Rollie smacked him.

"No one asked you, numbnuts," Rollie muttered.

Hawk had finished blinking and was now onto the opening and closing his mouth portion of disbelief. Finally, he found his voice.

"Do you want to run that by me one more time?" he asked slowly. "I'm sure I just heard you say you were in love with my sister."

I sighed. "Because that's what I said."

Hawk laughed, but it was humourless. "You mean you fucked her."

"What?"

"This is code for you fucked her, isn't it? You think if you tell me you love her that I'll… What? Take it easy on you?"

I shook my head. "No. It's not about the sex."

"You what?" he spat.

"Okay!" I cried. "Yes. I… We had sex–"

"How many times?"

"Dude, I don't think–"

"You're a fucking dead man, Grayson!" he roared and launched himself onto the table at me.

I let him grab my collar and swung him away from the table. We landed awkwardly and each got to our feet.

"I will kill you!" Hawk hissed and I believed him.

"It's different!" I yelled as I ducked his fist.

"Different? It's not fucking different." He swung again and I ducked again. "You knew the rules. I thought she was safe with you!"

"She is safe with me!" I winced as Hawk's fist whistled passed my cheek.

"You know," I heard Tank say. "I think we really need to develop healthier coping techniques. Better dispute resolution and all that."

"I dunno," said Rollie. "This has always worked for us."

I ducked another of Hawk's swings.

"An official dispute resolution policy would take forever to sort any shit out," Nico added.

"Let me hit you!" Hawk snapped at me.

I shook my head. "Not yet."

"What do you mean, 'not yet'?"

"I mean, you get to him me when you're okay with it."

"Hitting you might make me okay with it!" he paused. "I cannot *believe* the two of you went behind my back like this!"

"I can't believe you didn't guess," Nico quipped.

"Not helping!" I yelled at him as I grabbed Hawk's arm and shoved it away from me.

"It's kinda obvious now I think about it," Rollie mused.

"No!" Hawk said hotly. "No. There is no world where I'm letting my shit of a best friend date my little sister!"

"So, what does that say about you then?" I countered.

He pointed at me. "Don't make this about how I'm going to die alone because I'm equally undeserving of love. This is about you being unable to keep it in your fucking pants. It's Amber, Kit!"

Everyone in the room winced audibly. And not just because of how highly Hawk thought of himself.

Hawk hadn't called me Kit since he'd given me the Chaos nickname when we were sixteen. I'd been Christopher twice when he legitimately thought I'd died, but they were stories for another time.

"I'm painfully aware it's Amber, Pat. It only happened *because* it was Amber."

Hawk deflated somewhat. "What does that mean?"

"It means I wouldn't have fallen in love with someone else, mate. She's my one."

He scoffed humourlessly. "Sure. Until you get bored and move on like we always do!"

"I'm not moving on," I told him.

"You fucking will if you know what's good for you!"

I caught his fist in one hand and pulled him to me with the other one. "Dude, I am trying *really* hard not to swing back right now. But you're testing my fucking patience."

"Oh, your patience? My apologies. Because it's always about you, isn't it?"

I shoved him away. "I thought about this, Hawk. I knew what I was risking and I only went through with it because I was sure. She sees me. Not the fucking mask. Me, mate! She always has and you know it. Other than the four of you in this room, she's the one who knows me the best. Fuck it, she probably knows me better because I don't feel the need to be 'Chaos' around her."

"What? So now I don't know the real you?" Hawk scoffed and I saw the hurt in his eyes. "After every-fucking-thing we've been through?"

I shook my head. "No. Of course you do."

"But my baby sister suddenly knows you better?"

I couldn't help it, I exploded. I'd been intending a semi-rational conversation followed by a good old fistfight as dictated by the unwritten Grace Grayson bylaws. But I couldn't do rational anymore.

"Sorry I don't feel like snuggling up on the couch with you after a hard day of work! Sorry that your kiss doesn't make all those fucking horrible things we went through seem worth it! Sorry that your smile doesn't fucking light me up inside! Sorry that your arms around me doesn't make me feel worthy of someone's love for once in my fucking life!" I yelled at him. "I'm sorry I fell in love with your sister, Pat. I tried not to. But I want to be the guy who's worth her. Me. Not someone other shit-stain.

"I want to be the guy she comes to when she has a panic attack. I want to be the guy who's got her back. And I want her to be the woman who's got mine. Because God knows I love you fuckers more than almost everything in this world, but I think we all deserve a little romance in our lives!"

Hawk cleared his throat awkwardly, his fists falling by his sides. "If you wanted a candlelit dinner, mate, you just had to say so…" he said stiltedly.

The others were deadly silent. They'd never seen this side of me. Patrick Grace had been the only human to know I had feelings for about twenty-nine and a half years.

I huffed a rough laugh. "Forgive me, mate?"

Hawk looked at me. "I'm still going to have to hit you."

I nodded, because I knew that was his way of saying yes. He wasn't happy, but he'd forgive me. "Fair."

I took a step towards him and let him swing. I barely

even flinched. Tank, Rollie and Nico all did. Audibly.

"How about once for every time?" Hawk tried.

"I'm not telling you how many times I slept with your sister, dude," I told him, already feeling the bruise smarting on my cheekbone.

"One more, then?"

I shrugged. "I'll give you two as a sign of good faith."

Hawk gave me a single nod. "I can live with that."

He pulled back his fist and took another swing at my cheek. His third took me by surprise, landing square and sharp in my right ribs. Air whooshed out of my body as I buckled over and Hawk caught me to stop me dropping onto the floor.

"You hurt her and I'll do a fuck-tonne worse," he whispered in my ear.

I nodded, my eyes watering. "I'd expect nothing less," I wheezed.

"Good."

Hawk let me drop gently to the floor and I tried to get my breath back.

"Now the pissing contest's done, I'm interested to hear more about this dating business," Rollie said.

"Heads," Tank said and I looked up just in time to catch the ice pack he threw me.

I nodded to him in thanks and dragged myself back into my seat. The ice pack in my hand hovered between my side and my face.

"Ribs," Hawk said, kicking his chin at me.

"Yeah, he might need them late–" Rollie's sentence ended on an 'oof' as Tank pushed him out of his chair.

I looked to Hawk and we shared a smile. It was small given the circumstances, but I knew all would be forgiven. I'd probably never be off probation when it came to Amber, but I could live with that. If I did ever hurt her, I entirely deserved to be beaten to a pulp or whatever other horrible scenario my best mate was already planning for me.

"If we're all done, I believe Jefferson needs discussing," Nico said, sounding bored.

But, when I looked at him, he spared me a brief knowing smirk.

****

I was limping a little as I walked into the lift from the carpark.

"Mr Grayson!" Nigel yelped. "Exciting day, sir?"

I gave him a wry smile. "If you told your best mate you were dating his little sister, what do you think his reaction be?"

I could see Nigel understood my meaning perfectly. "He'd be pretty happy actually, sir. His brother-in-law's a real piece of work."

I nodded. "Good for you, Nigel."

"I presume Mr Grace wasn't quite so forgiving."

"Mr Grace," I said sardonically, "is better at forgiving with his fists than words, Nigel."

"Good for the sympathy, though, I presume, sir."

I laughed. Properly laughed. And I could see he was surprised by it. "Oh, Nigel. If you believe that, you clearly don't know Miss Grace very well."

The lift came to a stop and Nigel grinned. "She sounds perfect for you, sir."

"That she is. Night, Nigel."

"Night, sir."

I stepped out of the lift and dropped my bag by the study door. I winced as I took my gun off and put it away. I hadn't been game enough to open my shirt and see the damage Hawk had done, but he had a killer left hook so I knew I'd be sore for a few days.

But it was worth it.

Amber was sitting at her usual chair at the table, surrounded by her books and papers. I'd left her naked in my bed, and I saw she was wearing the t-shirt she'd stripped me of the night before. My cock twitched at the sight of it, but I figured he was a big boy and he could wait his turn.

"Hey," I said as I went to the fridge for a beer.

"Hey," she said warmly. "How was your day?"

I popped the lid and leant against the bench. "Same shit, different day."

"How was the…" She'd finally looked at me. "What happened?"

She got up and I held a hand up to her. "I told your brother about us."

All her concern melted to be replaced by a barely

restrained laugh. "You what?"

I nodded as I took a sip and walked around to her. "I told your brother I was in love with you."

"And he hit you for that?"

I smirked. "He may have guessed there was more to it."

"He *may* have?"

"Okay. He did."

She got up and came around the table to look at me close up. Her fingers hovered gingerly over the welt forming under and around my eye. "And all you got was a black eye?"

"And a shot to the ribs."

She winced, but there was no sympathy, only humour, in it. "Ouch."

I nodded. "He actually flew across the table to murder me."

Amber snorted as she tried not to laugh. "No? Really?"

I nodded again. "Scout's honour. It was pretty impressive."

"But you told him you're in love with me?"

If there was a time to act coy, it was now. "I might have."

"Were you, per chance, going to tell me?"

I shrugged. "I don't know if I'm ready for it."

"You're ready for Pat to try to kill you but not for…?"

I shrugged again. "You might not be ready to say it back. I wouldn't want to pressure you."

She laughed. "No. No pressure," she said expectantly.

I looked down at her. "Why is it always the guy's job to

say it first?"

"Is that your problem?"

"I currently have quite a few problems."

"Fine." She fought a smile. "Hey, Kit?"

"Yes, Amber?"

"I love you."

I fought a smile to stay in character. "You love me? I mean, I love Hawk–"

"I'm devastatingly in love with you."

"Devastatingly?" I chuckled.

She nodded. "Yes."

"Why devastatingly?"

"Because I'm devastated you were too wimpy to say it first."

I put my beer down and picked her up. Her legs almost got around my waist before I shook my head and had to drop her back down.

"Nope. Bad idea," I grunted through my apologetic smile.

She put her hand gently over mine on my ribs and she smiled softly.

"You might have to carry me to bed," I told her.

Those violet eyes shone. "How about we get you changed first and maybe get you some ice."

"I've had plenty of ice. I want something else," I said as she led me to the bedroom, letting me lean my arm around her shoulders.

"How about you do what you're told and maybe you'll

get a treat."

"You know, I like bossy Amber."

"Good. You're stuck with her."

"Perfect."

"Really?"

"Yes. Because I don't just like her, I'm *devastatingly* in love with her."

She rolled her eyes, but she was smiling. "Are you going to behave?"

"I promise nothing."

"Christopher!" she sighed exasperatedly.

"Are you the treat?"

"I might be."

"Then I promise everything."

She laughed as she turned to look at me. "You sure about that?"

I looked at her and I knew I was sure. We weren't ready for rings or white dresses. Yet. But I felt certain we would be, more certain than I'd ever been about anything else in my life. Amber Grace was my one and I was hers. Everything else would fall into place with time.

I took her face in my hands and nodded. "Everything, baby. I want to give you everything."

"All I need is you," she said softly and my heart skipped a beat.

"Oh. Then, my job's done," I teased.

She laughed with me, then we both just stared at each other, smiling those goofy, in love smiles. Amber Grace was nothing I knew I needed and everything I wanted. If all she wanted was me, I had to be the luckiest guy in the world.

"I love you," I told her firmly. It felt like such a flimsy way to try to convey the depth of everything I felt for her.

"I love you," she replied and suddenly I got it.

I got it.

I got just what those words did. It wasn't a flimsy way to convey a depth of emotion that seemed bottomless. It *was* the promise. It held everything.

She was everything.

I wrapped my arms around her and promised myself I'd never let her go.

Grace Grayson Security

The Grace Grayson team all have their own story to tell.

Next up is Patrick. Read on for more info.

Hawk & the Lady

See what all your favourite characters are up to down the track and maybe meet some new ones in Carter's story.

LEAH
All I wanted to do was get a cosy cottage in the suburbs and live with my million cats. What I got instead was suitor after suitor paraded in front of me and the threat of a looming engagement. So, what else was a girl to do?

PATRICK
If there's one thing that makes a guy reconsider his womanising ways, it's seeing his best mate and his little sister settle down. I don't know a lot about ladies, despite my remarkable ability to play a part. All I know is there's always more underneath the mask, and there's only one lady who can tame this hawk.

Buy now.

Chaos & the Geek

Thank you so much for reading this story! Word of mouth is super valuable to authors. So, if you have a few moments to rate/review Amber and Kit's story – or, even just pass it on to a friend – I would be really appreciative.

Have you looked for my books in store, or at your local or school library and can't find them? Just let your friendly staff member or librarian know that they can order copies directly from LightningSource/Ingram.

If you want to keep up to date with my new releases, rambles and writing progress, sign up to my newsletter at https://landing.mailerlite.com/webforms/landing/y1n6q2.

Follow me:

Thanks

This was my first public foray into the whole adult romance business and it was as terrifying as it was exciting. I did PLENTY of research (not at all for pleasure, no 😊) but that didn't mean I knew what I was doing. So my first thanks go to you, the reader, for taking a chance on this book and I so very hope you enjoyed it.

Thanks to Anna T for being the first (vaguely, lol) impartial person to tell me that I'm not terrible at this adult romance stuff. I did a dance of extreme happiness when you sent through your first lot of feedback. It sucks we live so far apart – I'm going to make it over to visit one day!

A significant lack of thanks but a lot of appreciation to my husband even though I had to sit through his merciless teasing in regards to my first "sex" book.

And I need to make note of an apology to the whole family for not writing under their preferred penname. I'm just far too lazy to build up a whole other platform. I'll always be Glitorus Clittertits to you all.

My Books

I'm working on my adult list, but you can find out about what I have planned at my website, as well as have a look at my older YA books;
www.elizabethstevens.com.au/after-dark.

About the Author

Writer. Reader. Perpetual student. Nerd.

Born in New Zealand to a Brit and an Australian, I am a writer with a passion for all things storytelling. I love reading, writing, TV and movies, gaming, and spending time with family and friends. I am an avid fan of British comedy, superheroes, and SuperWhoLock. I have too many favourite books, but I fell in love with reading after Isobelle Carmody's *Obernewtyn*. I am obsessed with all things mythological – my current focus being old-style Irish faeries. I live in Adelaide (South Australia) with my long-suffering husband, delirious dog, mad cat, two chickens, and a lazy turtle.

<u>Contact me:</u>
Email: contact@elizabethstevens.com.au
Website: www.elizabethstevens.com.au
Twitter: www.twitter.com/writer_iz
Instagram: www.instagram.com/writeriz
Facebook: https://www.facebook.com/elizabethstevens88/

www.ingramcontent.com/pod-product-compliance
Lightning Source LLC
Chambersburg PA
CBHW011159190726
48286CB00009B/2850